SIGNS OF COURAGE

Love Signs - Book Two

HANNAH KANE

Published by Blushing Books
An Imprint of
ABCD Graphics and Design, Inc.
A Virginia Corporation
977 Seminole Trail #233
Charlottesville, VA 22901

Hannah Kane
Signs of Courage

Print ISBN: 978-1-63954-034-1
v1

Chapter 1

As Lydia's eyes slowly opened, she smiled happily when she saw the branches of the apple tree leafing out just outside her bedroom window. The sun was coming up on the beautiful Wisconsin May day that was her wedding day. Lydia was actually going to marry the man she had fallen so deeply in love with just last fall.

She still had a hard time believing it was real. Cade McCauley was the head-turning, handsome man whom Lydia had met when their jobs put them together on the construction site of which he was the foreman. There had been an intense spark right from the beginning, but the path to their engagement was not smooth. One of the biggest problems was that Lydia, who had lived almost entirely in the context of her hearing-impaired twin sister, was completely inexperienced in relationships. Though she was a twenty-three-year-old teacher when she met Cade, she might as well have been fourteen for all she knew about dating, relationships and, certainly, sex. Her inexperience fed her insecurities about the idea that Cade could be interested in her. That lack of confidence had caused

1

her to behave immaturely at times and Cade would not stand for that.

Additionally, as they came to know each other better, Cade's dominant nature presented itself and Lydia discovered that, although she considered herself independent, Cade's take-charge manner brought out a submissive side that she had not known was there. This had her mightily confused. She found herself annoyed yet aroused. She found that when he spoke sternly to her and even when he spanked her like a little girl, her libido went wild. She didn't understand these conflicting feelings and her confusion almost ruined the relationship. But Cade helped her to understand that he cared deeply for her. He explained that his protective behavior was part of him and it had risen to the surface immediately on the day he met her. Cade had been raised in a family where his father was the head of the household and though his parents rarely argued at all, he knew that his father's word was final and his mother respected that. He knew he might have a hard time finding a woman who would follow his lead in these times, but that was what he hoped for and what he thought he'd found in Lydia.

Lydia had almost no experience with sex, so over the eight months of their time together, Cade had taught her by gently and persistently taking her to earth-shattering orgasms in many different ways. Lydia often found herself floating in what she thought must be heaven. She had come to desire him so much that she felt, at times, she had become wanton.

Cade found Lydia an eager student who was almost always ready to follow his lead into new—for her—sexual adventures. He found her inexperience and innocence a powerful aphrodisiac. She was nearly always on his mind and if she was within reach, Cade needed to touch and hold her.

Part of the success of their blossoming relationship was

based on the fact that Cade's dominance sought a woman with submissive tendencies and Lydia was perfect for him. He had made it clear to Lydia that her health and safety were of paramount importance to him and that if she took risks, there would be consequences. Lydia had been surprised when Cade laid down rules for her to follow and was shocked he actually put her over his knee, bared her bottom and spanked her—hard. After experiencing several painful and embarrassing spankings, Lydia began to understand how serious Cade was about her welfare. Confused about how she "should" feel about Cade's treatment, Lydia confided in her best friend Sarah, who was also raised in a household of dominant men and seemed to know about these things. She helped Lydia understand that getting a spanking was not in any way the same as abuse and that it generally indicated that a man cared for a woman very much and wanted to keep her safe. Lydia had come to understand that, though she could not tell Cade that it was okay to spank or punish her. It was also not going to be a deal breaker.

Lydia was small, just 5'2" to Cade's 6'3", and young, twenty-three to Cade's thirty. Lydia was also so innocent that his need to safeguard her ratcheted up. Cade was attracted to her unique beauty and she soon became very special to him when he watched the skill and compassion she used when working with hearing-impaired students on his construction site. Lydia was used to being a protector for her hearing-impaired twin but Cade's care and attention to her own health and safety were all new to her. A dangerous incident, in which Lydia had been hurt and also nearly kidnapped and assaulted, set the foundation of their relationship. Lydia surrendered to her complicated feelings for Cade, and Cade discovered that Lydia was the woman he wanted forever.

And now today, she would declare her love for him by

becoming his wife. Though Lydia had moved into Cade's large and beautiful home outside of Madison, they decided to spend the night before their wedding traditionally apart. Lydia felt alone waking up without his strong, warm body next to her so she decided to get up. Her twin sister, Lola, had come home from school at Gallaudet University, a school for those who are hearing-impaired, in Washington DC, to be her maid-of-honor. Lola was staying with Lydia in the house their father had bought for them when they went to undergrad school in Madison. She had not been able to be with her sister at all throughout the school year and was thrilled to be together with her again.

Lydia smelled coffee brewing and padded out to the kitchen where her beloved twin sister was starting breakfast. Her heart skipped a beat as she watched her sister busily scrambling eggs. As Lola's back was to her, Lydia waited in the doorway to be noticed. She did not want to startle Lola, whose hearing impairment would not allow her to know anyone was in the room. When Lola turned to see her, she ran to Lydia, threw her arms around her and then began using sign language. Just as they had while growing up, their fingers flew in conversation.

"I can't believe today is your wedding day!" Lola signed, jumping up and down. "Are you happy?"

"Oh, I can't believe it either, Lola! And I am happier than I ever thought possible. You know I love Cade very much."

"I can tell," signed Lola. "I see the way you look at each other and touch each other. It looks like love." Lola reached for Lydia and the girls hugged each other and rocked back and forth. "Now sit down and let me feed you a wedding breakfast before we begin to get you ready," Lola signed with a great big smile on her face.

The twins ate and "talked" giddily for about an hour

when, at noon, the doorbell rang. It was Lydia's best friend Sarah, who was also going to be a bridesmaid. They would spend the afternoon helping each other get ready for the wedding which was being held in the early evening.

Cade wished he had never let Lydia talk him into spending the night before their wedding apart. He had become so used to sleeping spooned against Lydia's naked body and perfectly heart-shaped bottom. He would never agree to a night apart again! Cade had slept restlessly when he slept at all, and as soon as the first rays of sun filtered into his bedroom, he decided to get up and work out, as that would usually clear his mind for the day. But not today. Not on his wedding day!

If anyone would have told him a year ago that he would find the perfect woman or that he would absolutely need to make her his own by marrying her, he would not have believed it. Neither would he have believed that such a remarkably beautiful, intelligent, fun loving *and* submissive girl would cross his path. But she did—in the form of one Lydia Lang.

Their meeting had been serendipitous. Cade's family owned a construction company which took charge of a charity build every other year called Home for Everyone. It was a community project, led by Cade and his brother Connor, to build a home for a low-income family using area volunteers. Last fall, as a new build got going, a group of hearing-impaired students who had also taken a yearlong construction technology class, came to volunteer with the hope they could be taken on as regular employees for the duration of the build. This was a pilot program at Three Rivers High School. Because the students were hearing impaired, an American Sign Language (ASL) teacher would accompany them. Lydia was that teacher. Looking back, even though Cade had doubts about the success of this unlikely project, he would say that he fell in love with Lydia at first sight. Their relationship did not go down a traditional path and there were barriers, but in the end, he believed they were meant for each other. He was eager to put a ring on her finger and keep her with him always.

Chapter 2

C ade and Lydia had tried to keep the wedding simple. They both wanted a smaller wedding, with a rustic setting. As it turned out, there was a wedding venue not five miles from Cade's home called Sandy Knoll Farm. A large old barn had been perfectly restored into a charming place to hold the ceremony, meal and dancing. If the weather permitted, and in Wisconsin that was always iffy, guests could spill outside onto lit decks and gazebos placed around the three-acre yard and gardens. They had visited Sandy Knoll soon after their engagement and Lydia had been enchanted. They chose their wedding date that night.

Now, as Cade, his brother, and his cousin waited with the minister at the front of the ceremony area, the sunset became visible through the dozens of expansive windows designed to let the outside in. As the sun went down, the lights inside and out began to come up and their twinkling made the scene magical. The bridesmaids slowly made their way down the aisle as the strings played quietly. Lydia's twin sister Lola and her best friend Sarah looked stunning in their form-fitting, strapless, soft jersey dresses in a soft rose color. Lola was

Lydia's identical twin. Only those who knew them well could tell them apart. Cade saw many of the men in attendance noticing Lola and though she was accompanied down the aisle by Cade's younger brother Connor, Cade had noticed that his cousin Rory had monopolized Lola at the rehearsal dinner. Now Rory stared at her as she made her way past him down the aisle.

Sarah, Lydia's best friend and bridesmaid, was a very attractive woman with a mane of blonde hair and deep brown eyes. She had an outgoing personality that shone through her brilliant and ready smile framed by dimples. Cade's brother Connor had become attracted to her months ago when she came to help Lydia interpret ASL at the building site. Their relationship was moving along at almost the same speed as Cade and Lydia's had. Connor's eyes were glued to the beautiful Sarah as she came down the aisle with Rory. They smiled meaningfully at each other.

Cade considered himself a cool customer—not easily rattled—and he maintained a rugged composure as he watched the bridesmaids come down the aisle, but as soon as the string quartet switched to Pachelbel's Canon in D and he caught a glimpse of his raven-haired girl in her stunning wedding dress with a veil demurely over her face to her shoulders, it was all he could do to hold it together. Lydia's dress was a simple soft jersey that hugged her lovely shape. It was the very palest of pink, which enhanced her porcelain skin. Though the dress had long sleeves, it allowed her shoulders and neck to be bare. The look was sexy and innocent at the same time. There was a very short train as Lydia was so petite, she had not wanted her dress to overpower her. There were iridescent beads sewn around the neckline and shoulders as well as the sleeves that gave Lydia the look of a fairy princess sparkling in the ethereal lights.

Cade actually made a choking sound that only his brother

heard but Connor leaned over and said, "Keep it together Bro. She needs you."

Cade took a deep breath, locked eyes with his bride and smiled reassuringly at her. Everything went smoothly after that including their vows, which included the word "obey" at Cade's insistence. Later, Lydia could remember very little of the party that followed. She moved as if in a dream, wondering if she would suddenly wake up and find that she had not just married Cade McCauley.

The well-planned reception was going just as they had anticipated but for one problem. Lydia's hearing-impaired sister Lola had flown in for the wedding on her own and though she was with their father and brother, Lydia found herself reverting to her old lifetime role of protector and companion. Lydia was checking on her constantly. Was she sitting alone? Were people including her? Was she happy? Cade had never seen them together but he understood that this was not healthy. When he noticed that she was ignoring other guests to check on her sister over and over, he finally grabbed her arm and moved to the edge of the room.

"Lydia, I know you are worried about your sister having a good time, but I don't think she needs you every minute. Your dad and brother are here and I've seen Sarah signing with her a few times. She looks just great and I think she is having a good time. Do you think you can let her manage on her own for a while?"

Lydia bit her lip, clearly struggling. "I don't know, Cade. This is the way we have always been together. She needs me."

Cade looked over at Lola. She was dancing with his cousin Rory and they seemed to be fine. In fact, he had seen Rory with Lola a couple of times now, even though Lydia was always interrupting them. Even now, she was stealing nervous glances their way.

"All right. Listen, Lydia. We need to cut the cake and say a few words of thanks to the guests. You need to be with me for a while now. I don't want you running to check on Lola."

Lydia looked a little panicked. "But, Cade…"

"No buts," he said as he moved his hand down to cover her bottom. "Do you want to get in trouble on our wedding night? Because that's where you're headed if you don't mind me on this. Do you understand?"

She lowered her head and said, "Yes, Cade. I'll try."

He put his finger under her chin and tipped her face up for a kiss. That got everyone near them teasing and calling, and Lydia had to laugh.

And Lydia did try, but Cade had to keep a close eye on her, as a couple of times she tried to sneak away from him to check on Lola. Finally, Cade took Sarah aside and explained what was going on. He asked if Sarah could see that Lola was not ignored and was having a good time. Sarah was the only other person besides Lydia who could communicate with sign language. Sarah was happy to help. Lydia's relationship with her sister was a little intense. It was something they would have to work on together. Cade was relieved that Lola was going back to school in a couple of days while he and Lydia were on their "honeymoon" at the family cabin up north. They would leave the next day and tonight, they would unwind at home.

It was only about 11:00 when Cade noticed Lydia slowing down. She was getting tired. It had been a full week of family gatherings, the rehearsal and dinner, and of course, the wedding. Besides, all he could think about was being alone with her again. Even one night apart, had been too long.

"Hey, baby," he said into ear during a slow dance, "how about we get ready to go? You look gorgeous in this dress but I'm dying to get you out of it."

Lydia blushed sweetly and said, "I was hoping you'd say that. All I want is you. Can we go now?"

"Well, you're going to need to change. I'll let the family know we are leaving and then you can throw that bouquet. Connor will bring the truck up and we can escape."

When Lydia stole a glance toward Lola, Cade grabbed her arm and said, "Cake. Now."

After throwing the bouquet—straight to Sarah—they made their final goodbyes, and when Lydia had a hard time leaving Lola, Cade picked her up to deposit her in the truck that had been decorated for the short trip back to his house. Lydia was so tired that her eyes began drifting shut on the ten-minute drive home. It was a good thing Cade had thought of a Plan B for their wedding night.

Chapter 3

Lydia heard the truck door open and felt Cade unbuckle and lift her out. The cool May night roused her and she realized that she had fallen asleep on the short way home from their wedding reception. She was ashamed of herself. She had been so looking forward to finally spending the night with her husband—oh, she loved that word, husband—and now she had fallen asleep. What must he think?

"Oh, Cade! I'm so sorry! I can't believe I fell asleep. Put me down. I'll be fine now."

"Now, Lydia, you know I am a traditional man, and I want to carry my bride over the threshold of the home we will share together. Besides, it's no wonder you are exhausted. It's been a long week of stress for you and I don't think you have been sleeping well. Never mind that you had maybe a few too many glasses of champagne tonight."

Lydia pouted. "Please don't scold me tonight, Cade. It's our wedding night!" she said as she put her arms around his neck and raised her face up to kiss him.

Cade opened the door and returned her kiss as he held her

in his arms. As he set her down he said, "Welcome home, Mrs. McCauley," and kissed her until she was breathless. "Let's get you comfortable," he added as he led her to their bedroom. Cade sat on the high king-sized bed and drew her between his legs. "Turn around, baby, and let me tackle those buttons."

Her wedding dress had a long row of buttons that reached from her neckline almost down to the swell of her bottom. Cade began to work on them as Lydia began to pull the veil and combs out of her hair. As the dress slid to the floor, she already felt so much more relaxed, but she was so very tired.

As Cade began to continue to undress her, she became irritated. "Cade, I can do this myself!" she said as she pushed his hands out of the way. "I don't need help!"

"You're going to get ready for bed without me—on your wedding night? I don't think so," Cade said as he continued to remove her underdress.

"Aargh!" shouted Lydia as she stood there in her bra, panties and thigh high stockings and stomped her foot. "I said I could do this by myself!"

Cade took charge immediately. In one swift move, he had her trapped over his knee, hands held in the small of her back and panties at her knees. He administered about a dozen hard smacks and watched as his red handprints decorated her pristine bottom. Then he held her there with his hand covering her backside and said sternly, "You, little girl, are overtired and behaving like a spoiled child. You know that is exactly how I will treat you unless you can pull yourself together. What have you got to say?"

Lydia was already crying, "I'm sorry Cade. Maybe you're right, I am very tired. But now I am ruining our wedding night by making you mad and getting a... well, getting spanked. I don't want this! I'm sorry!" she sobbed.

Cade gently rubbed her pink bottom and sat her up on his lap. "You haven't ruined anything, my love," he said reassuringly. "I think maybe we should get you in a bubble bath and bundle you up in bed for a nap."

"A nap? On my wedding night! Oh no, Cade, please don't make me do that! I'm sure I'll be fine after a shower. Please?"

Cade looked down at his weepy little bride who had placed one hand imploringly on his chest while her other one rubbed her sore bottom. She looked adorable, but Cade believed he should begin as he meant to go on, so he would have her mind him now. "Everything will be all right, baby. We'll get some sleep and wake up later with energy to do whatever you'd like. No one is going to bother us for a whole week. Understand?"

Lydia nodded her head hesitantly.

"I'm afraid without some rest, you will continue to be ornery and I would have to give you a real spanking that you would not forget so soon. You don't want that, do you?"

"No, Cade, I don't want a spanking at all," she said as a few tears escaped down her cheeks.

"Then you need to be good. I'll draw you a bath while you wash off your face and get your hair put up. You'll feel so much better then. I promise."

Lydia was disappointed not to wear the filmy negligee she had bought for her wedding night, but after her bath she was definitely ready for some sleep. Cade popped her into one of his t- shirts that was laid over a chair in the bedroom and tucked her in. Her eyes were already closing but she protested, "You're not getting in bed with me? I don't want to be alone tonight!" And once again, there were tears.

"I'll be there soon, baby. Just get comfortable while I shower and lock up."

"Oh. Okay," Lydia replied, already sounding sleepy.

Cade came to bed about fifteen minutes later to find Lydia just how he wanted her—sound asleep. He looked down at his wife's angelic face and tried not to think of all the things he would do to her when she woke up.

Chapter 4

When Lydia began to wake, the clock said 3:30 am. Remembering the night and day before, she was suddenly wide-awake. And there was her handsome husband sleeping peacefully beside her. The full moon shone in the patio window of their bedroom, so she propped herself on her elbow and lay studying this man she now called husband. His profile was strong and the stubble on his face and neck made her want to reach over and stroke him. His broad shoulders and expansive chest were bare and muscled. Really, he was irresistible.

Lydia crept stealthily out of the bed to use the bathroom. She ran a brush through her wild hair, cleaned up a little and then, after taking off his shirt, she smoothed her favorite body lotion all over her body. She was cold now so she moved quickly back into the bed beside him without touching him. He had rolled over, facing her now, so when his eyes popped open and his deep voice said, "Trying to escape, little girl?" she was startled.

"Oh! You scared me! I didn't know you were awake."

Cade pulled her close to him. "I always know where you

are, baby. You're freezing! Let me warm you up," he said as he flipped her over so her back was to his front and enveloped her with his warmth. She couldn't help but snuggle in.

Cade groaned, "Oh, baby, you smell delicious. I want you —now!"

Lydia giggled and said, "Well, I'm awake now and here for your pleasure, sir."

Cade reached over to turn on the bedside lamp as he wanted to feast his eyes on her perfect body. Then he moved one hand to cover her breasts and worry at her nipples until they were erect and hard. His other hand crept down and cupped her mons. Lydia's breath hitched. He leaned down to apply kisses all over her sweet backside and then said, "Oh, baby, your naughty little bottom is still pink from that spanking you got last night. You know that when you don't mind me, I will pull down your panties and spank and paddle you until you are bright red and raw—every time. Right?"

The fact that when he talked to her like that she became damp and aroused still puzzled Lydia, but it was happening now. "Yes, sir," she said as he placed a large finger at her entrance to find her wet and ready for him. Desire coursed through her as she continued, "I'll be good, Cade."

"How about this instead of a spanking?" he said as he pushed his finger in to find her clit.

It was there waiting for him and as he rubbed it just right, Lydia began to moan and squirm. "Oh, yes, yes, yes, Cade," Lydia cried out as he momentarily removed his finger and flipped her over onto her back. "Please, Cade, don't stop!"

"Spread your legs, little girl. I have no intention of stop-ping," Cade said as he replaced his finger over her ready nub and leaned over her to suck gently at her nipples.

Lydia could feel herself escalating and her breathing was already coming in short pants. "Cade! Hold me! Please! I can't…"

"Go with it, baby. I've got you. You are so beautiful."

Lydia was almost beside herself now but had not reached the peak.

"Baby, I want you to come. Now. Or I'll turn you over and remind your bottom what it feels like to get spanked."

That did it! His words were sometimes as powerful as his actions and she broke apart in his arms, crying out his name over and over until she caught her breath and said with passion, "I love you Cade."

He could wait no longer and after he kissed her eyes and forehead and heard her breath return to normal, he ordered her again to spread her legs and put them up over his shoulders. He really didn't know how long he could hold out and didn't want to embarrass himself.

When he positioned his cock at her entrance, his sweet girl smiled up at him and said, "I need you inside me, Cade. Please!"

With a deep groan, he pushed himself in, waited for her to accommodate him and with a final thrust, had her filled to the hilt. While Lydia's breath became ragged again, he moved slowly and then more quickly. The sound of her moans and whimpers drove him wild and before he really wanted to, he was filling her with rush after rush of his seed. When he had calmed, he rolled back and pulled her with him to lie on top of him, still impaled—both of them fully spent.

Lydia laid her cheek down on his chest where she could hear his heartbeat slowing and thought this was as close to heaven as she would ever be.

Chapter 5

One of the reasons Cade and Lydia chose their wedding date in May, was because the school-to-work pilot program they had both been involved in had wrapped up. The house project was all but finished and the students had received grades on their yearlong internship. The pilot had been successful, with Cade as the construction manager and Lydia providing ASL interpretation for the hearing-impaired students. They had received local, statewide and even national media attention and corporate sponsors were stepping up to continue the program in the next year. So before Cade went back to more traditional work in the busy summer season and as Lydia finished off the last few weeks of the school year, there was a natural break that would allow them a week for a not-too-distant honeymoon.

Cade was anxious to take Lydia to his family's "cabin compound" up near Eagle River. It was peaceful, beautiful and extremely private, as the McCauley's owned all the land around Eagle Nest Lake. Cade's great-grandfather had purchased a large lot on the lake and built a cabin for his family, and through the years the family added to the property, rebuilding an eight-thousand square foot master cabin, with state-of-the-art amenities that could accommodate two large families. Later, two other smaller cabins were built so that four groups could be together but separate when enjoying "up north" vacations. This early in the season, there would be no one at the lake and very few tourists in Eagle River or Minocqua, yet a few places would be open in case they wanted to eat out.

Lydia had never been to this part of Wisconsin and was impressed with the breathtaking beauty of the forests and lakes. Cade found her enthusiasm endearing, but she wanted to stop and take pictures of everything. Cade finally put a stop to that, telling her it would take all week to get up there if they kept stopping. She pouted a little but when Cade gave her the "look"—which she now knew did not bode well for her bottom —she let it go.

They drove on a lane through the forest until suddenly the cabin, beach and lake burst out in a clearing. It was so stunning that Lydia gasped. "Oh, Cade, I had no idea it would be this... this..."

"Big?" he offered.

"Well, this magnificent. Does all of this belong to your family? This is hardly a cabin! It looks like twenty people could stay here. Who takes care of all this when you're not here? Is there a boat? Can we—

Cade laughed. "Hold on, baby, we've got all week here. I'll tell you all about it. Let's just get settled in first." Cade was gratified to see Lydia so delighted with the place that was the source of so many family memories. He was already picturing their own family building traditions here.

Inside, Lydia was reminded of the design of Cade's own house that was a large, open-concept log cabin with dramatic two-story windows and breathtaking views. This cabin was much like that but larger. There was a huge common area with a giant floor-to-ceiling hearth and a state-of-the-art kitchen off to the side. On either side of the common area, were upper levels that led to separate family accommodations with three bedrooms and a bath and a half each. From the main area, two sets of patio doors opened onto a multi-tiered deck that stretched across the entire structure. Because the cabin was set high off the water, the view was near the tops of the trees with the lake peeking through. Lydia really thought she had never seen anything so lovely. While Cade brought in their luggage and supplies, she went out on the deck to stand in the day's waning sunlight. She was moved to tears by the beauty and when Cade came up quietly behind her to put his arm around her, she jumped. He saw her tears then and said, "What's the matter, Lydia? Are you okay? What happened?"

Then she did begin to cry as she explained, "You happened! You married me! And now we're together—here, in the most beautiful place in the world. It's almost too much."

Once again, Lydia's sincere innocence and honest emotions made Cade's heart stop. His love for her knew no bounds and he reached for her and kissed her like he never wanted to stop. When he finally pulled away, he said simply, "I will always love you, Lydia McCauley."

Chapter 6

Lydia had moved in with Cade after the Caruthers brothers had tried to hurt her, in retaliation for being fired by Cade Brothers Construction. His protective instincts, already heightened as he was falling in love with her, made it impossible for him to leave her alone in her house each night. When she moved in, it became clear that the two of them were not only compatible but truly loved each other's company. They were able to talk easily about topics from politics to what to make for dinner. They respected and cared for each other. And the sex was, well, the sex was explosive! Cade had taken Lydia's virginity and taught her the deep pleasures of making love. Her innocence and willingness to be somewhat submissive to his dominant nature convinced them both that they had found their lifetime mates.

So as they arrived home from their honeymoon up north, they both expected life would settle back into a comfortable routine. But it was not to be.

They had been working together every day since last fall. Now that project was over and though there may be another one for the beginning of the next school year, for now there would be transitions for both of them.

Lydia would finish the last two weeks of the school year working mostly in early childhood classrooms, teaching preschoolers how to use sign language to help them communicate. She might also have to spend some time writing reports required by the grant that funded the pilot construction project.

Cade and his brother Connor had bid on several large projects—two private homes and one commercial building. It looked like they might win all three. If that were the case, Cade would be working many more hours and would even need to hire more help.

The first week back after their honeymoon, Lydia was asked to give an evening presentation to legislators at the capitol on the success of the Three Rivers High School school-to-work program, and Cade's days were often ten to twelve hours. They went from being together 24/7 to ships passing in the night. Both Cade and Lydia were stressed, tired and irritable.

On Monday night, after a long day with preschoolers made longer with data collection and report writing, a dinner that Lydia had given some thought and time in preparing had been ruined when Cade didn't walk in the door until 7:00. She was angry that he hadn't called or even had his phone on. He apologized, but their evening together was short as Lydia fell sleep watching TV and Cade put her to bed but didn't join her until later when she was sound asleep. The next few days were about the same. They saw each other in passing. Only once, had they been awake enough together to make love. Cade was frustrated and Lydia missed his touch. She was so starved for his attention that she considered doing something that would make him angry. Maybe a spanking was better than nothing!

Lydia learned to be careful what she wished for as everything came to a head on Friday. They had argued Thursday night, and Lydia spent most of the time sulking and pouting about the long hours Cade was putting in. Cade tried to explain to her that the time of the year and the number of projects he was working on could not be helped. He told her it would get better, but she was tired and cranky. She stomped down the hall to their bedroom and it took all the patience Cade had not to follow her, put her over his knee and light a fire on her bottom to get her mind off his work schedule. On Friday morning when she barely spoke to him, he pulled her in for a lip-locking kiss that left her a bit dazed.

"Happy Friday, baby! We're going to have a peaceful weekend with just the two of us. I don't plan to let you out of our bed. I'll be home early."

Lydia was mildly placated, but later in the day when she remembered that she was giving a community presentation that night at the convention center, she decided to give Cade a dose of his own medicine and just come home late—not telling him where she was.

The presentation Lydia was to give was for the school board, city officials and some state legislators. She knew the school-to-work program for hearing-impaired inside and out. She had lived and breathed that program for the entire school year. And her colleague and best friend Sarah would be picking her up and accompanying her there for support, so she was not nervous. But when they drove into the parking lot, it was packed. And as they made their way to the ballroom where Lydia was to present, there were already perhaps two hundred people there, with chairs set up for double that. She was not the only person on the program, but she was shocked at the size of the audience. Now, she was a little anxious!

Sarah could see Lydia's trepidation so she hugged her and said, "You have nothing to worry about. You know exactly what you're doing, and I'll be right here. Easy-peasy! And isn't Cade coming to cheer you on?"

"Oh, Sarah, I didn't tell Cade about this except maybe in passing early in the week. We have had a terrible week—not seeing much of each other. There have been some communication breakdowns. He was so late a couple of nights without telling me, so I decided to pay him back. He doesn't know where I am."

Sarah could see that Lydia was beginning to panic, so she handed her a bottle of water and said, "Okay, just sit down and calm yourself. Big breath in and out slowly. Take a sip." Lydia followed her directions. "Listen, Cade is so proud of the work you do, and if you remind him that you mentioned this presentation to him earlier in the week, I'm sure he will get over his "mad" immediately. He would not want thoughts of him to make you nervous for your talk." In truth, Sarah thought that Cade would probably be furious and that her friend was most likely in trouble already. But there was nothing to be done right now.

The master of ceremonies announced the panel participants. There were four presenters who would talk about their programs, in hopes of gaining more support and funding, and then there was a period for Q&A afterwards. Sarah had helped Lydia edit a short video to go along with her talk. It did a great job showing how well the hearing-impaired students worked on the building site with Lydia interpreting for the students and workers.

Lydia was going to be the last presenter and it occurred to Sarah that Cade really should be there to see her. If she called him now, he might be able to make it in time to see her. She didn't want to get her friend in trouble, but really, that ship had sailed. Sarah decided to go for it and excused herself to go to the bathroom. Out in the hall, she dug through her purse to find her phone and found that she had five missed calls from Cade. He must be looking for Lydia. She knew she had to call him.

"Cade? "

"Where are you, Sarah, and do you know where the hell my wife is?"

"Yes, Cade, I do, but—"

"But nothing! You will tell me right now, or Connor will find out and you won't sit for a week. Am I clear?"

"Yes, yes, Cade. There's nothing to worry about. I'm with her. I'll tell you if you promise to calm down."

There was a pause and Cade replied in a measured voice, "All right, Sarah, I'm calm. Tell me where you are."

Sarah explained the entire situation to him.

"I'm on my way."

"Wait! Wait! Cade! She is already so nervous. The audience is larger than we thought and she has to wait to be the last presenter. Please don't let her know you are here. Please."

"Okay, Sarah, I'll just sneak in the back. And, Sarah, I'm glad you're there with her."

Sarah hung up and made her way back to her friend, feeling like she may have betrayed her. But she did what she thought was right. Sarah did wonder, though, how a man as large as Cade could ever "sneak" in anywhere.

Chapter 7

Even though Cade was fit to be tied when he set off to the convention center to find Lydia, he had stopped to change into some casual pants and a shirt that would be presentable in public. He began to speed but then realized that getting picked up would defeat his entire purpose of getting there in time to see Lydia's presentation. He worked to calm himself on the way, but in the end, her choice to not tell him where she was that night would not stand. When he got her home, he planned to paddle her until she was one sorry little girl who would never do anything like that again. No play spanking, no warmup, just a hard and meaningful session with her hairbrush, on her sweet, bare bottom. If he raised a few welts, that would be fine.

Cade didn't know anything about how long the program was or if he had missed Lydia's part, but he ran all the way from the back of the parking lot to the convention hall door. He found the right ballroom and quietly opened the door. He sat down in the back row. His timing was perfect because she was just being announced. Cade looked up and saw his beautiful girl making her way across the stage. She took his breath away every time he saw her after a separation—even a day at work. This week he had seen very little of her, and he realized that he missed her. She had her very long and very black hair pulled back into a thick braid. Tendrils curled around the edges of her high cheekbones and extremely fair face. She was wearing a short print dress with a flirty skirt and long sleeves. Her nude shoes on her tiny feet had heels taller than he had ever seen her wear. Her legs looked great! He was already proud of her and she hadn't even begun to talk. The audience chuckled when she reached the podium that was almost as tall as she was. Someone quickly brought out a step for her to stand on and helped her up on it so she could talk into the microphone. She handled it with grace, even making a little joke about how short she was. She looked comfortable and so did the audience.

The unusual school-to-work program that Lydia had helped to facilitate was a new concept so even though she was the last presenter, the audience looked engaged. She had confident stage presence that showcased her winning personality. Cade was falling in love all over again.

The video turned out to be a great addition, actually showing viewers how the hearing-impaired students were able to thrive and contribute in a meaningful way to work at the building site. There was plenty of footage of Lydia signing with students and he and Connor even made their way into the film, showing them working with students and with Lydia and Sarah. The applause at the finish was rousing and Cade almost stood up but remembered that he was "incognito." The fact that Lydia would have kept him from this reignited his anger a bit, but he was really glad Sarah had thought to call him.

As the Q&A session began, it seemed that everyone wanted to know more about Lydia's program. Cade proudly watched her field and answer all kinds of questions knowledgeably.

At one point an older man spoke up. "I own a contracting business and wonder how we could get involved in a program like this. Is there anyone here tonight from McCauley Brothers?"

Cade couldn't resist. He stood up and while the microphone was passed to him, he made eye contact with Lydia. She raised her hand over her mouth in shock.

"I'm Cade McCauley. My family owns the company in the video. I need to tell you that I was skeptical of this program when it was presented to me, but the staff at Three Rivers and most importantly this speaker, worked like crazy to make it work. We have nothing but good things to say about the students and the entire organization of the school-to-work program. It was such a success that we are working on making it happen again next school year. We are pretty sure it will work out, as this young woman and I worked so well together that just last month, I made her my wife."

There was a big "Aww" from the crowd and then thunderous applause. Cade looked up to find Lydia's face bright red, but she was smiling at him. And with that, the master of ceremonies called an end to the evening and Cade made his way through the crowd up to Lydia.

By the time he got up to her, Sarah was with her and the two of them were greeting people and answering questions. He could see his little girl was a bit overwhelmed so he took his place next to her, put an arm around her and said, "Folks, we appreciate the interest in the school-to-work program, and if you have any more questions, please contact the high school. It's been a long week and I am going to get these ladies home." He glanced at Sarah and signaled her to join them as they made their way through the crowd and finally out to the parking lot.

As soon as they got outside, Sarah said, "Connor is waiting for me so I'll see you two, okay? Great job Lydia!" And she was off before Lydia could say anything but thank you.

Lydia looked up at Cade and gave a little shiver.

"Cold, baby?"

"It was so warm before, I forgot to bring a jacket."

He put his arm around her and said, "Lydia, I'm so proud of you. You looked like a pro up there,"

Lydia bit her lip as she struggled with all the questions swirling in her head. How did Cade find out where she was? Was he angry? What happened now? But she gave him a quiet word of thanks and let him help her up into the truck where he buckled her in.

He grabbed a blanket from the backseat, covered her with it and kissed her on the forehead. "Let's get you home."

Lydia stayed silent most of the way home and, finally, when she couldn't stand it anymore, she blurted out, "Cade are you angry at me? Are you going to... spank me?"

He paused, seeming to consider his words and said, "You and I need to have a talk—a long talk. But everything can wait until tomorrow."

"Maybe after we talk, you won't want to spank me?" she asked hopefully.

"Don't hold your breath, little girl. You know you should have let me know where you were tonight."

Lydia gave a little moan and almost under her breath replied, "That's what I thought."

Chapter 8

It was already about 10:30 when Cade and Lydia got home. Their week had been challenging on many fronts and they were tired. Lydia began to make herself a cup of tea while Cade decided to shower. She turned the fireplace on and was just about to settle in when she heard Cade in the shower. They had not had time to be together at all this week and she was picturing his naked form with hot water sluicing down over his broad chest, muscular arms and powerful legs. When she thought about his taut ass, she made a decision. Lydia hurried down the hall to their master bathroom, discarding clothes every few feet. By the time she quietly opened the door to the steamy shower, she too was naked.

Cade was shocked when she opened the door to the shower and slowly approached him. It had been days since he had been able to feast his eyes on her perfect body, much less touch her. His cock sprang to attention as she smiled. "God, baby. You are so beautiful. Come here!"

Lydia approached him and laid her hands on his chest. He leaned down for a passionate, urgent kiss. As his tongue explored her mouth, he reached down, cupped her buttocks and lifted her legs around his waist.

"Oh, Cade! I need you," Lydia said breathlessly while he kissed her from her ear down to her collarbone as they both stood under the hot, streaming water.

He wouldn't be able to hold out long. He parted her folds with a finger and pressed up inside her. "Are you ready for me, baby?"

Lydia's breath caught, but she said, "We haven't been together all week. Can we please go a little more slowly?"

"You put me in a difficult position, my love," he said as he tried to position himself to have access to her.

Lydia wiggled out of his hold and put her feet on the shower floor. Now her mouth was at just the right place for her to lean in and lick and then nip at a nipple.

Cade drew a ragged breath. "Jesus Christ, Lydia! Where did you learn to do that?"

Instead of answering, she moved to his other nipple and repeated the action. She heard a groan come from deep inside him. "I want to make you feel good, Cade. See how nice it is when we slow down?"

"Slow down? Slow down?" he was just about bellowing now. Cade lifted her bottom again and she was forced to arrange her legs around his firm waist. Suddenly, he let go with one hand and brought it crashing down on her backside. He gave her three crisp smacks.

"Ow! Ow! Ow! Cade, please! Stop," she cried.

"Listen, little girl, as I think you already know, I call the shots here and "slowing down" is not to my liking when I haven't been with you for days." He spanked her again. "Are you ready to proceed, or would you rather slow down for a thorough spanking?"

Smacks on a wet bottom were extra painful and as she

reached back to rub away the sting, she said, "I'm ready, Cade. I'm ready when you are."

"Good to know," he said as he positioned himself at her entrance and entered her tight sheath. "Relax, baby, I'm almost there," he encouraged. But when she didn't, he said, "Maybe you remember what happens to little girls who don't mind. They get their naughty bottom spanked raw and then get to display it while standing in the corner. Do you understand?"

"Yes! Yes! Yes, I understand!" And with that, she relaxed and Cade slipped all the way in until he filled her. He gave her one more smack that had her hips moving and her breath coming in pants.

As for Cade, he knew he was nearly exploding and he could tell Lydia was in the throes of orgasm. She moved and cried out with abandon, reaching climax with a hoarse scream. Cade held her tightly and emptied himself into her until he was sated. She went limp, but he kept her impaled on him as their breathing began to return to normal. She threw her arms around his neck and hung on as he pulled out and carried her out of the shower.

Cade wrapped a warm bath towel around them both and sat her gently on the counter where he stood between her spread legs. He held her pressed against his chest as he carefully dried her. "Oh, baby, I missed you so much this week. I am not going to let our work keep us apart like this."

"No, Cade, I don't ever want to be apart from you. I love you so much!"

Cade grabbed some sleep pants for himself and one of his t-shirts for Lydia—his preferred attire for her when in their bed—then tenderly helped her brush and dry her long, thick mane. He carried her to bed where they both were soon sleeping soundly in each other's arms.

Chapter 9

The next morning, Lydia was awakened with a hearty slap to her bare backside. She squealed but Cade said, "Come on, sleepyhead. Are you going to sleep all day? Get yourself ready. I want to talk with you about some ideas I have so we don't have another week like the one we just suffered through. Hurry up! I'll make you some breakfast."

Cade had been up before dawn and had been thinking about changes he could make to his schedule so his days were not so long. He had some ideas, and after breakfast, they sat in front of the fire while he explained. He pointed out how the schedule of their lives had changed so dramatically when they came home from their honeymoon. They were no longer working on a build site together, but her responsibilities for promoting the school-to-work program had increased, keeping her very busy. His business had not only picked up as it normally would do in May, but the advertising that had inadvertently come from his work with Homes for Everyone and the hearing-impaired students had increased the visibility of McCauley Bros. Construction. He and Connor were swamped with more bids than they had ever had and were already working on the newest project.

"Look, Lydia, I'm sorry that I ended up working so many hours and leaving you alone without any warning. However, you had no excuse to try to "get even" with me by pulling that stunt last night. I was worried about you and actually a little hurt that you would not want me there."

Lydia was immediately in tears. "I am so sorry, Cade! Really, I am. Can you forgive me?" she sobbed.

Cade reached for her and pulled her onto his lap. "Don't cry, baby. Of course, I forgive you. But tell me, what do you think will happen if you ever do anything like that again?"

She didn't answer so he lowered his chin and raised his eyebrow. "Lydia. Answer me."

She hated it when he made her say what she knew he would do so she still didn't answer. But when he began to move her off his lap into a position over it, she said quickly, "If I do that again you'll… I'll… be spanked!"

He sat her up again and said, "Spanked is not the half of it Lydia. I will spank you first and follow it with a paddling. You many even end up with a naughty girl plug inside that bottom. Do I make myself clear?"

She was quietly crying now. "I promise I'll never do it again, Cade. I'm so sorry. I'll be good. I don't want to get paddled!"

He held her a while and kissed her head. "So let me tell you what I'm thinking." Cade went on to explain that he was going to call his cousin Rory. When visiting for the wedding, he had been complaining of a downturn in business in the Wausau location. Cade had flippantly suggested they close down up there and Rory join him and Connor in business down here. Now he realized that they could talk seriously about this consolidation, as his business was getting to be more than he and Connor could handle. He would call Rory today, to set up a family meeting in the next couple of weeks.

"Okay, but what can we do right now? Will you have to work ten-to-twelve-hour days all summer? Is there any way around that for now?"

"There is. I'm going to talk to Connor today about passing on one of the projects we bid on. That way we will just have two going at once. That number is common for us in the summer. I'll even hire a few more men to take some pressure off and I'm hoping Rory can bring some of his crew down here. My days are still longer in the summer, but we'll have to get used to that. Maybe we can take a week or two off to go up to the cabin, though. What do you think?"

"That sounds like a plan, Cade! It would make me so happy to be able to be with you every night and weekend." She put her head on his chest and snuggled into him.

"Now you tell me what your plan for this summer will be. I don't even know if you usually take the summer off, work part time, or what? What are you thinking for this summer?"

Lydia explained that she usually worked as an ASL inter-preter in early childhood classrooms for six weeks in the summer, but classes were only two hours each morning. This year it looked like she may be called on to do more work on the school-to-work grants for the next couple of years. She would hear about that this week. For now, she didn't know exactly.

They both felt better about going forward with a plan and as Cade moved in for a deep and meaningful kiss. Lydia, relieved that she had avoided a spanking, knew just how they would be spending their afternoon.

Chapter 10

It was the last week of the school year, and as the construction project they had worked on together was finished, Lydia spent all her time in the early childhood classrooms. She would probably continue to work mornings there during the six weeks of summer school but was waiting on word to also work on grant writing.

Cade and Connor had begun work on a large home about thirty miles west of Madison. It was the first of two large projects they were committed to for the summer. Their days would be long.

Thursday of that week was the last day of school. Lydia was helping other teachers pack up their supplies and take down their rooms at the early childhood center. After the students had gone home, Lydia heard her name over the PA being summoned to the principal's office. That was unusual in itself, but when she got there, she was surprised to find two strangers standing with the principal. One was an older professional woman who introduced herself as Jennifer Hyde and the other was a man she recognized as State Senator Jake Jacobi. He was a tall, good-looking man, perhaps around forty.

He was dressed impeccably, causing Lydia to look down at the old jeans and t-shirt she had worn to clean out classrooms. Lydia's principal and friend, Lauri, was smiling excitedly as she made introductions. Ms. Hyde was from the Office of Special Services at the capital and the senator was, well, he was the senator.

He smiled broadly at her and took her hand in both of his. "It's so nice to meet you, Ms. Lang."

"Oh, it's actually Mrs. McCauley now, but please call me Lydia," she said and, for some reason, felt a blush rising.

She thought she saw his eyes narrow at that information and he held her hand a little longer than was appropriate.

Lauri spoke up then and said, "It seems Senator Jacobi was at the presentation last week when you explained the school-to-work program, and he would like to talk with you, Lydia. You can use the conference room if you like." She motioned to the conference room door and then excused herself.

So, if he was at the presentation, he should have known that she was married! They sat and Lydia took a calming breath. "What can I do for you, Senator?"

Over the next hour, Ms. Hyde and the senator explained how impressed they had been with Lydia's presentation last week—her speaking skills, stage presence and ASL skills. The senator explained that several legislators now employed ASL interpreters when they did public events. This was generally arranged through Ms. Hyde in Special Services, but she explained that the senator had wanted to meet her himself, to see if he could talk her into training to become an interpreter for legislators.

"Does that sound like something you would be interested in?"

Lydia had always been intrigued by the ASL interpreters she saw working for speakers in person and on television. She would love to try that out but wasn't sure if this was the right time in her life to do it. Lydia worked to process all that had been said and knew she would need some time.

"I am flattered that you thought of me and I am very interested in hearing about the work. But this is a lot to take in so suddenly. I would have to know much more about the commitment, expectations and training. I really like the work I do now."

"That is understandable," said the senator as he leaned forward and put his hand on Lydia's forearm. "I hope you will consider meeting with Ms. Hyde to get the information you need. At first, I would request that you work with me and no one else. Then, as you become experienced, you could consider some others."

Lydia pulled her arm onto her lap while Ms. Hyde reached into her briefcase.

"Here is my card. Oh, and one more thing. The pay is seventy dollars an hour, and there are also benefits. I wonder if there is any chance you could come to the capital tomorrow for me to give you more details and the paperwork should you decided to join us?"

Lydia felt pressured, but what could it hurt to just go get more details? And seventy dollars per hour? Wow!

"I can be there after school tomorrow," Lydia said as the senator stood and flashed a dazzling smile at her.

"I hope Ms. Hyde and I can talk you into joining us. I look forward to seeing you again," he said as took her hand again. "I'll see you tomorrow."

And they were gone. Lydia sat back down while her brain swirled around what just happened. She was excited, flattered and confused. This was something she really needed to discuss with Cade.

But Cade was home much later than he wanted to be that night, and he'd had a stressful day on several fronts. Even though Lydia really wanted to tell him about her offer from the senator, she understood that it was not a good time. She had a feeling Cade might not be enthusiastic about the proposition, so she decided to wait until he was in a better mood.

The next morning, Cade was off early and was preoccupied, so she chose again not to tell him about her meeting at the capitol that day. She was disappointed, but was it a big deal? She was just going to find out details about the job. She had a little niggling worry that she should tell Cade all about this, but by the time she worked up the courage, he was gone. She justified that everything would be okay if she told him all about it that night.

Chapter 11

Lydia had never had to dress "business professional" before and she did her best with her most conservative dress and low heels. She gathered her hair into a modest low twist at the back of her neck and wore very little makeup. During the day, she had tried calling Cade a couple of times but it went to voicemail. She became irritated and decided that she was done trying to tell him and would just go ahead. She turned her phone off and made her way to the capitol.

She followed Ms. Hyde's directions to park near the east door of the capitol building and make her way to the rotunda where she would meet her. Lydia had never been inside the capitol building and the size and scale of every feature was a little overwhelming. Her heels clicked noisily on the tile floors and she could hear some voices echoing at the end of the hallway. It was late in the day, so there were not many people around.

She was just becoming a little anxious when Ms. Hyde appeared and strode toward her with an outstretched hand. "Welcome, Lydia! I'm so glad you found your way. Just follow me to the senator's office."

"Oh, I thought we would be meeting in the Special Services office to go over some details."

"Well, Jake—or I should say Senator Jacobi—decided that he wanted to meet in his office. I think he hopes you will be agreeing to work with him, and I think, too, that he would like to practice a portion of a speech with you today. "

Now Lydia was nervous. She had not planned on staying so long. But she said nothing. As if sensing her mood, Ms. Hyde said, "There's nothing to worry about. I assure you that Senator Jacobi is a gracious man and will put you at ease right away. Ah! Here's his office."

They entered and Lydia noticed it was a very large and well-appointed suite. There was a reception area, a conference room and an inner office that was obviously for the senator. The woodwork was finely carved and the windows covered in heavy shutters that were closed though the day was sunny. It seemed a bit oppressive. There was a seating area with two fluffy down chairs that matched a plush loveseat. Lydia could see the adjoining conference room and headed for it as that seemed like the most business-like place to talk.

"Oh no, dear," said Ms. Hyde with a chuckle as she motioned to the loveseat. "The senator likes his guests to be most comfortable. Please sit here. I'll go over some things with you and at some point Senator Jacobi will arrive to do a practice run with you. Are you ready to get started?"

Lydia was anxious and feeling sort of stupid. She had not asked how long this meeting would take. She should have. Neither Ms. Hyde or the senator had mentioned doing a practice round of a speech and it was already late in the afternoon. She had not told Cade anything about where she would be or when she would be home. He was going to be furious. She didn't have many choices, though, so she let Ms. Hyde begin to fill her in on pay, hours, protocol, procedures, and more. Somehow Lydia managed to take it all in.

Just as Ms. Hyde began to wind down, Senator Jacobi came in. He was dressed more casually than the first time she had seen him, but his clothes were expensive and showed off his trim and slightly muscular form. He flashed Lydia a smile and came right over to sit so close to her, their legs were touching. He took some pages from a folder and said, "Well, Jenny, is Lydia all filled in?"

"I've given her all the pertinent information, but I'm not sure she is ready."

"Not ready? She looks ready to me, Jenny—ready for anything," he blustered. "Have you ever seen such green eyes, Jenny? You're going to turn some heads in the conference, Lydia!"

He was like a bulldozer, but Lydia managed to say, "Thank you. Ms. Hyde gave me a lot of information and I need to think about this as a commitment. May I have some time?"

"Time? Sure, as long as we can meet tomorrow to go over an important speech I plan to make later next week. You can let us know tomorrow. Now, let's look at this practice piece. I need to get an idea of your pacing. Jenny, you can go. Lydia and I can take it from here."

Lydia was uncomfortable that she would be alone with him now, but Ms. Hyde seemed to take it in stride. "Great! Lydia, I'll get the paperwork ready for you to sign when you are ready, all right?"

"Okay," Lydia sighed.

Before she knew it, he had handed her some papers. "Read this over to see if you feel you can interpret the entire speech. When you're ready, we'll go through it as if it's the real thing."

Lydia began to read to herself. This was a pretty straightforward speech about a bill that was going up for a vote in the senate. Lydia understood it and thought she would be able to sign with no problem. However, the senator remained sitting quite close and read over her shoulder, interrupting her to point out phrases that she might not understand. At one point, he had both arms wrapped around her as he pointed things out. She could feel his breath on her neck.

She stood up quickly, moving his arms out of the way, and said, "Senator, I believe I understand what I am doing. Are you ready to begin?"

He laughed arrogantly. "No reason to get snippy, Lydia. Has anyone ever told you that you tend to overreact? Here now, you stand across from me so I can see you as I speak. A good ASL interpreter uses her whole body when she works."

Lydia tried to stay calm as her face turned pink.

"You are such an innocent, Lydia. It's going to be fun working with you."

He was so inappropriate, Lydia began to feel slightly nauseated. Maybe she should excuse herself to the bathroom and call Cade. But he would be so angry. What if he drove to the capitol and confronted the senator? What if the police were called? No. She would simply finish this practice and get out of there as fast as possible.

The senator began his speech, and Lydia began signing. Even though he spoke quite fast, she was confident that she was keeping up. Besides, she didn't want to stop him as she would be forced to stay longer. After several unnecessary interruptions, they were finished. Lydia was nervous and tired. She yawned.

Suddenly, the senator's demeanor changed completely. He looked angry. "Are you bored, Lydia? Is this work not exciting enough for you?" he said as he took a couple of steps toward her.

She forced herself to stay calm. "Of course not, Senator.

It's all very interesting. I just had a long day. I really need to get home now."

"That's too bad. I was just going to offer you a glass of wine. I thought maybe we could sit and talk," he said as he picked up two wine glasses from the cupboard behind his desk.

"Maybe another time, sir. I am quite tired." Lydia was desperately hanging on to her last shreds of calm. All she wanted to do was get to the door and get out of there. She picked up the small purse that was next to her. Her coat was across the room so she left it. She continued to think of ways to placate him. "Thank you again for taking the time to work with me tonight. I learned a lot. I look forward to working with you."

If she told him that he would never see her again if she could help it, it might set him off so she tried to casually walk to the door. He followed her, reached around and unlocked it. The door had been locked! He opened the door and then moved to trap her against the doorframe.

"I hope you don't mind me saying so, Lydia, but I find you just beautiful. I look forward to working together."

Lydia all but held her breath waiting for his next move. Blessedly, he stepped back and allowed her to leave.

"See you tomorrow, baby. And, Lydia!" She turned to look back at him. "Whatever fragrance you're wearing, always wear it when you're with me. It drives me wild!"

"Oh my God," Lydia whispered under her breath. *This man is crazy!* She took a deep breath and kept walking as normally as she could. She didn't know if he was still watching her, or worse, following her. Finally, she came to the rotunda and was close to the outside door. There were security guards there so she felt safer. As soon as she stepped outside, she yanked off her shoes and ran to the car. It wasn't until she was blocks away that she pulled over and burst into tears. She couldn't even let herself think about what could have happened to her alone with that clearly unstable man in his remote office in a huge empty building. She was so lucky to be safe in her car. Lydia knew she would not be lucky when she had to face Cade. He would be justifiably furious. But in truth, the idea of Cade's wrath—and even a spanking—seemed like nothing compared to what she might have faced with the senator. She took a few sips of water, caught her breath and steeled herself to look at her phone that had been turned off in her purse.

Oh God, there were a dozen calls from Cade in the last hour. The last one was just five minutes ago. She did not have the heart to listen to Cade's rant in voicemail so she braced herself and made the call.

Chapter 12

"**G**oddammit, Lydia! Where the hell are you? Are you all right? Goddammit!

"I'm so sorry, Cade. Truly. I—"

"Sorry! You're sorry? I come home—you're not here, your phone goes to voicemail—I have no idea where you are, what you are doing or when you'll be home? And you're sorry? Where the fuck are you? And you didn't answer me; are you okay?"

"I'm okay, Cade. I'm on my way home. I was at the capitol."

"You're fucking downtown, at night, by yourself? Goddammit, Lydia! Have you lost your mind?"

She had never heard him so worked up. Not even the night that she was beaten up by Daryl Caruthers. It seemed that no matter what she said, it upset him more, so she stayed quiet and waited. Lydia could tell he was trying to get it together.

"God, baby! I've been out of my mind with worry. I was just about to call the police. You're okay to drive? How long before you're home?"

"I am fine, Cade. I just had, um… it was an unusual experience. I should be home in about twenty minutes." She paused and added, "I'm so sorry, Cade."

"Just get home. *Now.* But drive carefully. Don't speed."

"I won't. I'll see you soon."

"You are in so much trouble, little girl."

"I know."

Lydia pulled up to see Cade actually pacing in the driveway. It would be funny if the situation weren't so serious.

As soon as the car stopped in the garage, he yanked open the door, dragged her out and held her in a bear hug for a long time. Then he grabbed her upper arms and brought his lips to her face. He kissed her forehead and then her lips repeatedly. When he held her away from him and looked her over checking for damage, he saw that her eye makeup was smeared. "You told me you were fine, but you've been crying."

"I've been crying because I'm so sorry I scared you," she lied.

"You're cold. Didn't you wear a coat?"

"No, I didn't," she lied again.

He wrapped a protective arm around her and led her into the house. "Do you want to take a warm shower or bath? When was the last time you ate something?" Cade was still caught in the throes of anxiety for her safety.

"I'll take a shower."

"And did you eat?"

Lydia opened her mouth but just stammered, "I-I didn't." She shook her head.

Cade ran his hand through his hair with exasperation. "Okay. Take a shower and get comfortable. I'll make you something." She nodded and turned as he finally let go of her. "Lydia, you really scared me."

Tears welled in her eyes. "I am so sorry."

In the shower, she again considered the plan she had

thought through on her drive home about how much to tell Cade about today. She had decided that telling him everything would be too much. For now, she knew he was angry that she hadn't told him about the job interview or about where she was going. He was beside himself about that. To also tell him how the senator had come on to her in that perverse way— that would have to wait. Or maybe if she just called Ms. Hyde the next day to say that she would not be accepting the position, she would never have to tell him. The senator was a respected public official. The incident was a he-said-she-said kind of thing and that never worked out well for the woman. And then Lydia was afraid of what Cade might do. He might threaten the senator, or worse, want to confront him. The publicity would be really bad for everyone concerned. No. For now, he didn't have to know. It broke her heart to keep anything from him, but what else could she do? She really couldn't tell anyone.

Lydia turned up the shower to as hot as she could stand, washed her hair and scrubbed every inch of her body, trying to distance herself from the memory of the senator's touch and lewd innuendo. She worked to put that experience out of her mind. She was going to have her hands full handling Cade's anger. So far, he had not scolded, lectured or threatened her with a spanking, but she was pretty sure he would be addressing her behavior.

She put on her pink, soft-as-silk lounging pajamas that were also deliciously warm and padded out to the kitchen. Cade was buttering toast and there was a bowl of chicken noodle soup waiting for her. As she watched her beautiful man moving around the kitchen caring for her, her heart grew heavy that she had faulted him for not being available to listen to her at the very moment she wanted to tell him and now, added to that, was the fact that she needed to keep something from him—lie to him. She wondered how she had gotten herself into this mess.

Cade came up behind her, put a hand on her shoulder and put the toast in front of her. Again, he kissed the top of her head and said, "Eat."

Lydia found that she was quite hungry and managed to eat the toast and soup quickly. She took a few sips of milk, set the glass down and looked up through her lashes to ask, "Are you going to spank me, Cade?"

"Do you think you deserve one?"

She hated it when he asked her that. There was no good answer. But this time she really did think she deserved it, so very quietly, she whispered, "Yes."

"I'm glad we agree because I do plan to spank you. But not until we talk. Let's go." He grabbed her hand and pulled her toward their bedroom. He sat on a corner of the massive bed and drew her between his legs. She knew from experience that this was his preferred position for her when he was going to lecture—then spank.

"All right. Let's hear the story. How did it happen that you decided not to tell me where you were or when you'd be home and you ended up downtown at the capitol after dark?"

She had to admit, it sounded pretty thoughtless when he said it like that. She took a deep breath and began with the senator and an assistant visiting school to ask if she would be interested in doing ASL work for legislators. She explained that she didn't tell him about it because he got home late that night and seemed tired and a little agitated so she thought she would wait. At this point she looked up into Cade's eyes waiting for him to say something. He still looked serious and stern but remained quiet.

She continued, "This morning, you were up early and there didn't seem to be time to tell you about it then, and when I called you a couple of times later, your phone went to voicemail." She paused. "So I thought... well, you seemed busy... I, um, turned my phone off then and decided to just tell you about everything later." Lydia knew how that sounded and she bit her lip.

"So you are saying that the fact that you didn't tell me where you were is my fault? Is that how you see it?" Cade asked incredulously.

Lydia was wringing her hands and really chewing on her lip now. "Well, sort of, I guess. I was disappointed that I couldn't tell you about what happened. I was flattered to be asked. I always wondered about what that kind of interpretation was like."

Cade took her hands to still them. "And the reason you didn't tell me is that there wasn't time? Really?"

"Okay! Okay! Last night, you were in a bad mood and tired and also I thought you might not like the idea of me looking at a new job—so I just didn't tell you! I thought I could do it myself and if I actually got an offer, I would have told you." Lydia was getting upset now and stomped her foot. "And I had no idea the senator would want to go through a practice run. I didn't know I'd be gone so long."

Cade grabbed her arm and gave her a little shake, "All right. Now you are being honest. But your reasons were still not a good excuse to keep me out of the loop and then scare me to death when I couldn't find you." Cade's voice was raised now as he continued. "That was a series of bad choices, Lydia, and I never want you to make them again. Do you understand?"

Lydia was already crying, but Cade was unmoved. He flipped her over his leg and pulled down her pants and panties in one move and then grabbed the hand she put back to shield herself. He held it in the small of her back and began smacking. Even the first few were bad and it took her a minute to get enough breath to scream. But she did! And she kept screaming as Cade's hand continued to spank over and over.

"Don't you ever, ever, do anything like that again! You could have avoided this by telling me the truth in the first place, but now you're in for it!" Cade did not stop spanking as he scolded and Lydia knew she would not be able to sit for a very long time. Her screaming was becoming hoarse when Cade finally stopped, laying his hand across her bottom and waiting while her cries became whimpers and hiccoughs. He grabbed some tissues and sat her back up on his lap. She hissed as her bright red bottom made contact with his jeans.

He wiped her nose and face while she said in a watery voice, "I'm sorry, Cade. So sorry."

"I know, babe. And you're forgiven," he said, holding her and rubbing her back gently. But I want you to go to sleep now." He took her bottoms off completely and laid them aside, as he believed having a bare bottom was a reminder for her, and tucked her under the covers. "You've had a long, bad day."

The last thing Lydia thought before she fell asleep was that Cade really had no idea how bad her day had been. And she didn't ever want him to find out.

Chapter 13

It was Saturday, so Cade let Lydia sleep. He rose up on his elbow to look at his beautiful wife. Her silken black hair was swirled all around her as she slept soundly. Her lush lips were even puffier in sleep and her high set cheeks were rosy. Even rosier, was her bottom. She was sleeping on her tummy in deference to the backside he had spanked and required she keep bare. There were no bruises, but it was certainly still red and sore looking—as he meant it to be. He never wanted to be as frightened as he was last night when he didn't know where she was. She was the most important thing in his life, and as he looked down on her gorgeous, sleeping form, his heart ached with love. But he left her there undisturbed to get rest he knew she needed.

The sun was high in the sky when Lydia finally woke up and stretched. She rolled to her back only to squeal as she remembered last night's awful spanking. Then her mind traveled back to the ordeal at the senator's office. She was so upset by it but still felt she could not tell Cade. Tears were forming in her eyes just as Cade came in.

"Hey, babe! You awake?"

He sat down next to her on the bed and heard her sniffle. Then he saw her tears. He wiped them away, assuming she was still feeling a sore backside. He continued as if she was fine. "Listen. Didn't you want to go to Dundee's nursery for plants? I've got some time today. I could help you with that. We could get something to eat on the way. You must be hungry."

She really was still too upset to be hungry but smiled up at him and nodded.

"Get yourself ready. I'll get you some coffee."

As soon as he left the room, she grabbed her phone and searched her purse for Ms. Hyde's number. The sooner she called everything off with the senator, the better.

"Hello, Ms. Hyde? This is Lydia McCauley."

"Yes, Lydia, hello! And you can call me Jenny, as I'm sure we will be working together."

"Well, that's why I called," she said with some hesitancy. "I'm afraid I won't be able to accept your kind offer."

There was silence for a moment on the other end. "Well, I am very sorry to hear that. And I know the senator will be disappointed as well. Can you tell me why?"

"I think this is just not the time in my life to pursue another job. The ones I have keep me quite busy. And as you know, I am newly married."

Ms. Hyde's tone changed. "I wonder if you understand that if you pass up the senator's offer to work together, you will probably not get called from the Special Services Office again. Are you prepared to give up a job that pays seventy dollars per hour?"

Lydia tried to hold her own. "I didn't know that, Ms. Hyde... Jenny, but, as I said, this is not the right time for me."

Now Ms. Hyde's voice became shrill. "The senator will be very disappointed. He took an instant liking to you. I am disappointed as well. But if you've decided, there is nothing I can do, I suppose. Just don't expect to be offered a job when the 'time is right'." That last bit was sarcastic.

Lydia was ready to be finished with the conversation. "I am sorry to disappoint you both. For now, I have things to do today so I must go." She hung up before she heard any more. Lydia found that she was upset. That woman was so pushy and it reminded her of how inappropriate the senator had been. The same sick feeling she had the night before came over her.

Just then she heard Cade call out, "Let's go, Lydia!

When he lifted her into the truck, she stifled a small groan as he put her in the seat. Her bottom was still sore and she was worried about the forty-five-minute trip to the nursery. Cade disappeared and came back with a pillow from their bed.

"Sit up, baby. This will help."

"I'm not going to use that! Everyone will see and know… well, know what happened!"

"No one will see," he said, laughing, "but if you'd rather not…"

She grabbed the pillow from him. "Okay, I'll try it." She was so embarrassed that she blushed bright red, but she moved it under her and it did help.

They decided to stop at an old-fashioned drive in where they could stay in the truck and eat burgers and cheese nuggets. Then they had a really good time choosing annuals, perennials and vegetable starters. They just about filled the truck bed and Lydia was delighted. She had not worked in a garden since before she and her sister left for college. She missed it—as she missed Lola.

Cade was relieved to see Lydia happy. They were home by midafternoon, so he unloaded all the flats near the areas where they would be planted. As he brought out the last load, Lydia was already happily placing plants where she wanted them. "You can't get this all done today, you know."

"I know. Just let me have some fun."

The afternoon sun made it a perfect day to be outside. Cade went in, fetched her a lemonade and brought it out where she was working. "Drink something, will you? I don't want you dehydrated."

"Oh, I'm not even sweating. But thanks." She took a big gulp and then noticed that he was holding out sunscreen.

"I want you to put some of this on if you're going to stay out here. Your skin is so fair. You must burn easily."

"Oh my goodness, you are such a mother hen, Cade! I'll be okay." He gave her a look that she recognized so she grabbed the sunscreen and began to apply it to her face and neck. "Are you happy now?"

"I'd be happier if I had you in bed right now," he said as he lifted her face for passionate kiss.

"Okay," she sighed, coming up for air.

"Later, baby. Connor just called and the client at the new build wants to show his parents around and he thinks we should be there. I'm going to run over there. But..." he grabbed her and kissed her again, "hold that thought."

Lydia went back to working in the garden as Cade drove out to meet Connor.

Chapter 14

L ydia was completely wrapped up in placing and then planting the plants and flowers they had just brought home. She lost track of time, but when she felt the gentle breeze become a little cooler, she looked up. She had probably been out there about an hour. She should go in, clean up and think about dinner.

Suddenly, she heard the patio door on the deck shut. Was Cade home already? She looked toward the patio but saw nothing. She straightened up the materials and tools she had been working with and headed to the back garage door where she could brush herself off and go into the kitchen. Lydia opened the door and called for Cade. No answer. She came fully into the kitchen then where she could see the entire great room. To her shock, there was a tall man standing with his back to her in front of the fireplace—and it wasn't Cade! She gasped as he turned around, revealing that it was Senator Jacobi. Immediately, Lydia felt a chill up her spine and her heart began to pound. Thinking back on how she had handled him the night before, she gathered her strength to sound calm. "Senator! What are you doing here?"

He held up some papers. "Oh, Lydia, remember that I told you we would need to meet today to go over this speech? And you left your coat in my office. I thought I would save you the trouble of driving into town to pick it up. I tried calling, but I see you left your phone in the house." And with that he pocketed her phone. Lydia could feel terror rising but fought it back.

"Well, let me wash up a bit and then why don't you bring your speech in here. We can look at it here on the island. Can I get you something?"

"I'd love a beer if you have one, but I'd rather work in here. We can sit on the couch and use the coffee table."

Lydia said nothing but washed her hands and face off and brought an open beer out to him.

"Here, Lydia. Sit next to me. We'll read through the speech together so your signing will go more smoothly. We need to present this next week."

She moved to the couch where he moved up so close that he was able to put an arm around her. "God, Lydia! You are a sexy girl. Your husband is a lucky guy. But here, let me read through it for you."

The voice in her head was desperately wishing Cade would come home *now*! She didn't care if there was a scandal. She didn't care about anything but getting away. The senator clearly had mental health issues, and she was afraid. She had no idea what he would do next. He began to read and asked her to follow along. As he read, his hand began to stroke her arm and then her back until she couldn't stand it and jumped up.

"Senator, can you keep reading while I begin dinner? My husband will be home soon."

The man stood up and Lydia could not discern his look. "I don't think he'll be home soon. The build he is working on is almost an hour away and he left just an hour ago. I was parked out on the road and I saw him leave. We'll have plenty of time. No need to start dinner now. In fact, I think we can go right to the speech. I'll read it and you sign. Stand over by the fire so I can see your whole body. Senator Jacobi had not let go of the wrist he had grabbed when she jumped up. Now his grip was becoming tighter.

"Senator! Sir! Please let go of me! You're hurting me!" Lydia was in a full-blown panic now. She had to get away from him.

Suddenly, she thought she heard the kitchen door to the garage open. Hoping upon hope that it was Cade, Lydia lunged toward the senator, and in his surprise, she was able to pull the hand still grasping her wrist up to her mouth and give it a powerful bite.

The shocked senator screamed, "Bitch!" and let go of her wrist but reached into his jacket and pulled out a handgun. Lydia tried to run around him to the kitchen, but he grabbed her.

"Oh no, Lydia, you're not going anywhere. I came here to fuck you. It's just you and me, baby!"

Then she screamed with everything she had, "Cade! In here! He's got a gun!" She let out a wild scream at the same time she saw the senator's fist connect with the side of her head. There was an explosion in her head, then she was falling... and falling, until everything went black.

Chapter 15

Cade and Connor had decided to go together to the building site and were almost there when the client called and apologized for a family emergency that would not allow him to meet. The men proceeded to the site to check on the progress and make sure their timetable was still a go. On the way home, Cade suggested that Connor come over for dinner. Lydia was making her famous ribs and he was going to fire up the grill for the first time this year. He agreed and Cade tried calling Lydia. He was not concerned when she didn't answer because he had left her working happily out in the garden. Her phone was probably in the house. She would be happy to have Connor.

As they approached the long driveway to Cade's house, they noticed a BMW parked oddly at the side of the road just before the turn to the driveway. It looked like someone had pulled over in a hurry and left the car. They stopped to check it out. The car was locked and there was nothing to give them any idea as to the owner.

"Let's search some and then maybe call the police. This is pretty strange," Cade suggested.

They split up and walked in opposite ways down the road and into the woods, calling out for someone to answer. They gave up after about twenty minutes. Then Connor said, "Does Lydia have any friends who might be visiting?"

"I don't think so, and besides, why would they park out here?" Cade answered. Suddenly, a bad feeling came over him. Lydia was home alone, probably out in the yard, and that car out here was weird. Something was wrong.

"Okay. Maybe I am overreacting, but let's leave the truck here and walk up to the house. You go in the door that leads to the lower level in back and come up that way, and I'll go in the garage to the kitchen."

"You think there's someone in there with her?"

"I don't know, but I have a bad feeling."

The men approached the house without speaking and went to opposite doors. Cade had just put his hand on the doorknob when he heard Lydia scream. Someone was in there and they had a gun. Cade's blood froze when he heard Lydia. There was a hunting rifle in a cupboard near him in the garage. It wasn't loaded but the intruder didn't know that. Cade grabbed it and rushed the door.

The sight that greeted him was one he would never forget. Lydia was lying still on the floor, her hair spread out wildly underneath her. She had clearly been struck in the face and there was blood coming from her mouth and nose. Standing over her, was a tall, powerful man with an unhinged look on his face and a gun pointed straight at Cade.

"Drop the rifle, now! Or I'll shoot."

Cade put the rifle down on the floor next to him. He was desperate to get to Lydia so he took a couple of slow steps.

"Don't move. I'll kill you both!"

Cade saw Connor sneaking up behind the man with a baseball bat, so Cade started talking to cover Connor's steps. "Look, I don't know what you're doing here, but I need to see if my wife is all right. Let me check on her, " he said as he slowly moved toward Lydia.

"Stop!! Don't come any closer!" he said as his hand with the gun shook. "Lydia's in love with me. We had this meeting planned. You didn't know anything about it, did you? You're so stupid. You're not good enough for her. I'm a senator—"

And that's when the bat Connor was wielding connected with the senator's head, making a sickening crack. The man stumbled and fell over the table in front of the fireplace and he was out.

Cade rushed to Lydia who seemed to be regaining consciousness. "Oh my God! Baby! Lydia! Don't move; I've got you," Cade said as he cradled her head. "Connor, call 911 and then call Anson." Anson Carter had been Cade's best friend growing up, and now he was a detective with the Madison Police Department. Cade knew he could completely trust Anson to handle everything well.

"Cade, oh thank God! He hit me." Lydia's speech was a bit slurred as it caused her great pain to moved her jaw and her lips. "I'm sorry, Cade. I didn't tell you. I didn't tell you!" And then she began to cry.

"Shh, baby. There's nothing to be sorry for. I'm here and so is Connor. You're okay. Don't talk right now." Cade knew it was important not to lose it, but he couldn't help the sickening dread he felt. He was here with his sweet wife who had been hurt badly—and there was something she hadn't told him.

Connor saw tears forming in Cade's eyes and he moved over to Lydia to distract them both. "Hey, little sister, Cade invited me over for some of your famous ribs. I guess that's not happening tonight, huh?"

She smiled a half smile but said, "No, Connor. I can't. I'm so, so tired." She closed her eyes, but they knew they had to keep her awake.

"Lydia, stay with me, baby. I need to see your beautiful

green eyes. You know I love those. Wake up, honey! I love you!"

Lydia struggled to stay awake as they heard the sirens getting closer. Senator Jacobi was still unconscious. Connor had explained that there were two injured and unconscious persons so they sent two vehicles and two teams. The EMTs burst through the front door and began to tend to both Lydia and the senator. Though it was painful, Lydia could answer some questions about her injury. Other questions would be left for the police.

Before the EMTs moved either victim, Anson Carter raced through the front door and began immediately assessing the situation. Connor greeted him and told him all that he knew. Anson turned to Cade to hear one of the EMTs say, "Cade, you've got to get out of the way, man! Just back off a little. I know you're worried, but I need to assess her."

Anson and Connor moved in and talked Cade into coming into the kitchen where Anson could get Cade's statement. Cade was beside himself so Anson told him that he had what he needed for now and he should just go with Lydia in the ambulance and they would talk further later. Based on what he had heard, Anson cuffed the senator who was still out cold and accompanied him to the hospital. He wanted to be there when he woke up to find out what the hell had been going on.

Chapter 16

I t took hours for Lydia's injuries to be assessed and treated. It turned out that while no bones were broken, the blow to her face had been powerful and there were cuts and bruises. She also had a mild concussion so they wanted to keep her overnight for observation. Lydia was allowed to sleep because she had been carrying on a conversation and her pupils were no longer dilated. However, she would need to be awakened every few hours to be sure she could be roused. Cade stayed with her every minute, but finally, he fell asleep in the recliner in her hospital room.

When Anson came in at about 11:00 the next morning, he found Lydia awake but saw his exhausted friend sleeping with his head on his wife's hand.

"So, who's the one being treated here?" Anson said with a chuckle.

Lydia shushed him, but Cade woke up, wiped his hand over his face and said, "You ass, get out of here."

Lydia was appalled. "Cade, Anson is here to help us. Be nice!"

"Yeah, okay, baby." He stood and smoothed her hair off her face. "How are you doing this morning, baby?"

"It hurts, Cade," Lydia answered honestly.

He leaned down and very gently kissed her forehead. "I'll call for more meds, just rest." Then remembering that Anson was there, he asked, "What do you need, Anson?"

Anson moved to the other side of the bed. He took Lydia's hand and asked gently, "How are you doing today, Lydia? Do you think you can tell me about what happened?"

Cade stood up defensively. "Look, Anson, she's in pain and it's difficult for her to talk. She hasn't even been able to tell me about it yet. Do we have to do it now?"

"Well, Senator Jacobi has lawyered up. It's pretty important that we get Lydia's side of the story. I hate to say it, but he has money and power. He's also one of the sleaziest guys I have ever known," Anson said seriously. "I know this is painful, but I just don't see a way around it."

Lydia interrupted, "I can do it. Please!" She looked at Cade. "Can I just try? I'll go as long as I can and then rest. Please, Cade. I want to get this guy."

Cade reluctantly agreed, and the three of them settled in while Lydia told her awful story.

After the nurse came in with some pain meds, Lydia was able to talk to Anson for about forty-five minutes before she had to stop. She was aware that as she told Anson about the way the senator had spoken to her and touched her in his office, Cade was hearing it for the first time too. When she told them that the senator had asked her to stand up across from him so he could watch her whole body, Cade had to stand up and then began pacing in agitation. As she continued with more inappropriate things the senator had said and done, Cade's face turned so thunderous that Lydia, feeling this was all her fault, finally stopped her story. Both she and Cade had tears in their eyes.

When the doctor came in to give instructions about releasing Lydia to go home, Anson took his leave, saying they could continue the next day if they were up for it.

Lydia was happy to be going home, but Cade said very little on the way there. He stopped to get her one of her favorite milkshakes, as she could not chew solid food, and when they got home, he insisted on carrying her into the bedroom. She started to complain that she wanted to be in the great room, but Cade looked so worn out that she stopped. He helped her change, got her some water and tucked her into their bed. Lydia was exhausted and fell asleep immediately.

Cade, though relieved to have Lydia safe and at home, had been shaken to his core upon hearing about how the senator and his aide had come to school to recruit Lydia for an ASL position and then talked her into going to the capitol the very next day to "practice" with the senator. And the story about how he trapped her in his office alone and came on to her—it enraged him. He wanted to punch a wall! He faulted himself for not protecting her.

Lydia had said that she didn't tell him about the senator at all because he had not been around and she had no opportunity. He had worked late the night after the senator's school visit and had left early the next morning, so there was no time for him to listen. That was on him. But she also said that she didn't want to tell him for fear he would not allow her to pursue the opportunity. That was on her. He thought they were clear on the fact that transparency and communication were of utmost importance. They needed to have a long talk about that.

But for now, Cade saw his job as taking care of Lydia's every need. He called his brother to say he would not be at work for a couple of days. Connor suggested that maybe now was a good time to see if their cousin Rory could come down and begin to help out as they were hoping we would end up joining McCauley Brothers.

Cade and Connor had always been close, but this experience reminded Cade how important family was when the going got tough. Connor had actually saved their lives!

Chapter 17

By Sunday, Connor's girlfriend, and Lydia's best friend, Sarah had heard about what happened and was frantic to see Lydia.

But Connor had not allowed it yet. He knew that Cade and Lydia needed time together and Lydia needed more time to heal. Sarah found this completely unreasonable. She needed to see her friend and she was pretty sure Lydia needed her as well. She decided to drive out to their house the next morning after Connor went in to work, to see if she could somehow get in to see Lydia.

She had brought a bouquet of peonies and she rang the doorbell hopefully. Cade answered the door, and though surprised to see her, invited her in.

"Cade, I'm so sorry to bother you, but I've been so worried about Lydia," she said as tears formed. "I know she is hurt, but do you think I could talk with her for just a little while?"

Cade had wanted Lydia to rest all day. His need to protect her was in high gear. But Sarah was so sincere and he knew she cared about Lydia, so he said, "All right. Let me see if she is awake." He came back and said, "She's awake and wants to see you but, Sarah—I have to tell you she looks a little rough. Her face is bruised, swollen and cut. And talking for any length of time is painful for her, so this has to be short. Okay?"

Sarah nodded and followed Cade to the bedroom. There Lydia lay, her small form on that gigantic bed. Lydia turned to greet her and Sarah had to stifle a gasp. The entire left side of her face was covered with dark and swollen bruises. Her lip on that side was twice its normal size and was cut. Her eye was swollen shut. It took everything Sarah had not to burst out in tears, but she held it together and with a cheerfulness she didn't feel, she said, "Oh, Lydia, I'm so happy to see you! I've been so worried. But I can see Cade is taking such good care of you."

Lydia motioned for Sarah to sit on the bed next to her. "Oh, I'm so glad to see you too. Please forgive me if it's hard to understand me. This lip is really in my way," she said as she tried to smile.

Sarah couldn't hug her or touch her face, so she took one of her hands in both of hers and just held it. At that point she could not keep some silent tears from streaming down her face.

"Don't cry, Sarah. There is nothing broken. I will be fine— in a few days. Everything will be okay." Then to Cade, she said, "Baby, can you get something for these flowers?"

When he left, Lydia whispered, "God! Am I glad to see you, Sarah. Cade is glued to me. He won't let me out of his sight or out of this bed, and he's driving me crazy. Please talk to me about something normal."

So Sarah entertained Lydia with some work gossip and a couple of stories about herself and Connor. She actually got Lydia to laugh. "Speaking of Connor," she said as she brought her face close and spoke conspiratorially, "Connor forbade me to come to see you. You know I don't mind pretending he's the boss but 'forbid'—I'm not having that shit! I needed to see you with my own eyes!"

Lydia couldn't help but laugh. Sarah was so irreverent! "But I don't want you to get in trouble."

"I'll be fine. *If* he even finds out, I can handle Connor."

Suddenly, a voice from the doorway said, "Oh yeah? You think you can handle me? We'll see about that! What did I tell you about coming out here?"

Connor stood there, looking angry, and for all Sarah's big talk, her eyes grew big and she bit her lip. "What are you doing here?" she asked with some sass.

"The bigger question is what are *you* doing here?" he said as he came to put a hand on Sarah's shoulder and look down at Lydia. "I told you that Lydia needed her rest, and you had to sneak over here," he said, giving her a little shake. "We're going to have a discussion about this."

Lydia piped up, "Oh, Connor, please! Please don't be mad! I'm so happy to see her. It's just what I needed. I'm so glad she came."

Connor smiled at Lydia but reached down to grab Sarah's arm and pull her to stand next to him. "I'm glad she cheered you up but defying me and sneaking around behind my back is going to have some serious consequences," he said to Lydia but kept his eyes on Sarah. "Time to go."

Sarah blushed, but Connor was already dragging her out the door. She called back, "I'll see you soon, Lydia. Get better!"

Lydia could hear Connor scolding her all the way to the front door. Even though Connor was more easy going than Cade, she thought Sarah had pushed him into a probable spanking. She hoped he would let her come again.

Chapter 18

I t was just a few minutes later that Lydia heard a commotion coming from the great room. She heard the raised and agitated voices of Connor, Cade and Sarah. She had to find out what was going on and it seemed they were not going to come and tell her. Lydia sat up on the side of the bed slowly. It made her face throb, but she stood up anyway. She grabbed her robe and made her way to the front of the house. She was a little unsteady, but she could hear all three people talking at once.

Lydia peeked around the corner and saw Connor and Sarah peering out the front windows and Cade behind them on the phone. They all seemed frantic.

"What's going on? Connor, what is it?" Lydia asked through her cracked lips.

Cade, still on the phone, glared at her and pointed back toward the bedroom.

Lydia tried to push her chin out, which caused her to groan in pain, and stand her ground. She took advantage of the fact that Cade was occupied and that he seemed upset, to skirt around him and approach Connor and Sarah. "What is it? Please tell me what's going on?"

"Okay," said Connor, "but come and sit down." They led her over to the couch and joined her—Sarah next to her and Connor positioned in front of her on the ottoman.

"We don't exactly know what is going on, but there are a lot of reporters out on the lawn. It probably has something to do with the senator being arrested. Cade is calling Anson to see what we can legally do to get them out of here."

"What?" Let me see." Lydia tried to get up, but Sarah stopped her.

"Lydia. No. You can't go near the windows. It's not safe!"

Just then Cade put his phone down, looked at Connor, and said, "Anson is coming out with several squads to get these assholes out of our yard. So there'll be county and city cops here soon." Then he turned to Lydia. "What the hell are you doing out of bed?"

"Cade, please," she implored as he moved in to pick her up. "I was scared. No one told me what was happening. Please don't make me get back in that bed. I'm so sick of it!"

Cade was not deterred and continued down the hall with her in his arms. He called out to Sarah, "Sarah, can you come back here and keep Lydia out of trouble?"

Sarah jumped up and followed them into the bedroom.

"All right, stay away from the windows and turn your phones off," Cade said as he closed the blinds. Then he sat next to Lydia and took her hands. "Everything will be okay, baby. But it's really important that you mind me today. Do you understand?"

Lydia bit her lip out of habit and then winced.

"Sarah, can you get Lydia her pain meds? Connor and I have to make some plans, so please stay back here for now." He came over and kissed Lydia on the head then went to join Connor.

After Lydia took her meds, she felt like she really needed a shower. She begged Sarah to help her and even though Sarah was worried about what Cade would say, she decided it was best to keep Lydia happy, comfortable and distracted. Sarah supported Lydia in the shower and talked her into not getting her head wet at all. Then she helped her dry, dress in fresh and cozy sweats and get back in bed. The activity had worn Lydia out and she fell asleep almost immediately.

When Sarah went back out to the great room, Cade and Connor were huddled with Anson and another man in uniform. She didn't want to bother them but she wanted to know what was happening out in the yard, so she headed for the front window. She was stopped in her tracks by Connor's bellow, "Goddammit, Sarah! I told you to stay away from the windows!"

It seemed like an overreaction to Sarah, but she understood that the men were upset. Still, she huffed and sort of stomped over to sit in front of the fireplace.

Later, Connor came over, picked her up and settled her on his lap. She struggled a little but then gave in. "I'm sorry I yelled at you, babe. But this is such a big mess! And I just want you and Lydia safe. Understand?"

She nodded and asked, "Can you tell me what's going on?"

"It's pretty complicated. Why don't you wait for Lydia to wake up and we can tell you together? We'll probably be here most of the day, as will Anson. There will be a security detail keeping the reporters off the lawn, but there's nothing we can do about them camping out on the road. A lawyer Anson recommended will also be coming out."

"What can I do to help?"

"That's my good girl," he said, kissing her temple. "You can see to Lydia, keep her company and make sure she's comfortable. Maybe you could also see if you could rustle up some sandwiches and coffee. We'd all appreciate that."

"I'd be happy to," she said as she kissed his cheek and got up.

"Oh, and I don't know if I need to tell you this or not, but it would not be wise for you to cross me, or Cade, today. I don't want to hear any arguing or sassing. Got it?"

She wanted to say something smart, but this really was not the time. She didn't think Connor would have any problem taking her into one of the bedrooms and paddling her ass—no matter who could hear.

"Got it," she said with uncharacteristic meekness.

Chapter 19

I t took about a dozen officers from both the sheriff and police departments to get and keep reporters away from the McCauley house. But by the time Lydia woke up midafternoon, they were all corralled out to the road. The road was public property so they could not be forced to leave.

Cade had gone in to check on Lydia, to find her waking slowly. He poured a glass of water as her greeted her. "How do you feel, baby?"

"I'm hungry for a big, fat cheeseburger, but I'm afraid all I can manage are soups and ice cream." Then remembering how this day had begun, she sat up rather quickly and said, "What's happening? Is everyone still here? Are the reporters still out there?"

"The reporters have been beaten back to the road and there are only a few left. But Connor and Sarah are still here. So is Anson, and we're going to need to go talk. Anson and the lawyer he has suggested need to hear our stories. I'd do anything not to put you through that again, baby, but the senator has a lawyer and is trying to sue us."

"What? He intruded into our home, assaulted me and

would have... well, he might have raped me if you and Connor had not come home! He is suing *us*? I don't understand!"

He gathered Lydia up next to him with his arm around her. He put the unhurt side of her face on his chest and gently rubbed her back. "Shh, shh, shh. There's nothing he can do to us. We know the truth. But he is going to be aggravating. You need to be as strong as I know you are and remember that I will always be with you. Do you think you can talk with Anson and the lawyer—I think his name is Jackson? If you can't, we can maybe put it off until tomorrow."

"No!" she answered emphatically. "I will do anything keep that horrible man from doing anything like this to anyone again!" When her head began to ache, she quieted and added, "Besides, Cade, I can do anything if you're with me."

"I love you, Lydia McCauley," he said as he kissed her unbruised cheek. "Get yourself ready, but if you need to stop, or get tired, we can call it off."

The mood was somber as Lydia, Cade and Connor began to recount the story for Anson and the lawyer, whose name was Jackson Graves. Retelling the story was difficult, and Lydia began to cry when Cade told how he had come in to see her lying there with a man who was holding a gun. Cade nearly lost it when Lydia remembered as much as she could of the way the senator had talked to her. When pressed to use his exact words, she had to repeat 'I came here to fuck you,' and Cade actually roared, stood, knocked the chair over and began to pace like a wild animal. They stopped then so Connor could guide his brother outside and calm him down. When they came back, Cade put Lydia on his lap and held her protectively. She did not argue.

Jackson began calmly, "I know this has been difficult for all of you and I appreciate your honesty. But now I have to tell you what I am hearing from the lawyers the senator has hired.

Because Lydia was alone with the senator, what he said and did is a he-said-she-said thing. Much will be difficult to prove. However, he was in your home uninvited and was carrying an unregistered gun, so we can begin there."

Cade's face was getting red and he ground out, "Begin? Begin? I want to finish this guy!"

Anson interrupted to say, "Look, Cade, I get how angry you are, but Jackson knows what he's doing. I've seen him take down powerful guys in a courtroom. But you need to stay as calm as you can and let him work."

Lydia reached up, stroked Cade's cheek and said, "We can do this, Cade. Right?" Then she turned to Anson and the lawyer and said, "You said that there's no proof of what he said to me, but I think there is." Lydia wiggled off Cade's lap and retrieved her phone from the charger. It had been returned to her at the hospital after having been found in the senator's possession. She found the app she wanted, worked her way through prompts and looked up. Everyone looked puzzled except Anson, who was smiling. She pressed 'play' and the voice of the senator could be heard saying, "God, you are a sexy girl, Lydia…" And then every awful word of the senator's conversation when he and Lydia were alone in the house could be heard, ending with her scream. Lydia stopped the recording and went to put her arms around her husband whose face had turned ashen. For a moment, no one said anything.

Then Sarah spoke up. "Lydia you are a genius—a brave genius! Then she turned to the lawyer and said, "So there's your evidence?"

Jackson shook his head. "Lydia, it's amazing that you had the presence of mind to give Alexa the startup word to record the senator, but I am sorry to tell you that recordings like this are not admissible in court."

This time both Cade and Connor exploded, "What the

hell? We have him threatening her, and us, and it can't be used?"

Jackson worked to appease them. "Please listen. It doesn't mean no one will hear it. The judge will hear it when we ask to have it admitted as well as the senator's lawyers. It will be out there. We also have photos of Lydia that show the effects of his attack on her. No one can deny those."

Cade spoke. "So you're saying the senator will continue to lie and may be believed?"

"I would be willing to bet he will most certainly continue to lie *and* try to blame Lydia, and Connor, for hitting him. *But* this may not go to trial. There is a lot of negotiating to do. I hope you will trust me to do that. I will keep you posted on everything and we can make decisions together. I know this has been an ordeal, but I would ask that you not get discouraged," Jackson said as he looked at Cade and Lydia. Then to everyone, he said, "Please remember to be discreet about this entire case when out in public. Just don't talk about it. Reporters will try to trick you into making statements and curious people will badger you. Don't give in. It's really important. Understand?"

Everyone at the table nodded their heads.

Jackson and Anson left, promising to check in tomorrow, and security arrangements were made to keep a team on their house until the case was settled. Soon after, Sarah and Connor said good night and Cade and Lydia were relieved to be alone again.

They had not made love since the attack and Lydia craved Cade's attention. So, though she was tired, she took a shower, shaved—everywhere—and put on his favorite body fragrance. She crawled in bed naked and waited. And waited. He didn't come. She would have to go get him. When she went into the dressing room to get the short nightgown he favored, she looked at herself in the lighted mirrors. While her lip was not bleeding, it was still swollen to twice its size and the bruises on the side of her face and neck were turning the sickening yellow green that bruises do before they begin to fade. Her eye was open but still swollen. She looked pretty ugly and it suddenly occurred to Lydia that maybe Cade no longer found her attractive. Why hadn't she thought of that? All of her old insecurities came rushing back. When they first met, she could not understand how such an unbelievably handsome and all-around great guy could be attracted to her. It had taken a lot of work, and even a spanking, to persuade her that he thought she was perfect for him. Now she remembered those bad feelings. They were back. She was a fool to think a pretty night-gown and favorite fragrance could overcome her truly unattractive bruised face. She felt now that she was foolish to wait for him in bed. She couldn't bring herself to go to him. So she just crumpled to the dressing room floor and cried.

And that's where Cade found her ten minutes later, still on the floor—and still crying. Panic gripped him. Was she hurt? What had happened? His protective instincts went into over-drive and he swooped down and picked her up in one move, holding her close and murmuring soft and comforting sounds as she curled into him, still crying her heart out. He sat her against the pillows at the head of the bed and moved his hands over her. "Where are you hurt? What happened, baby?" He grabbed tissues and began to gently mop her face.

She came to life then, batting at his hands and saying, "Stop! Stop! Don't look at my face anymore. I know it looks hideous. I didn't know why you haven't made love to me since... since the attack, but I realize now that I don't look the same. And I miss you so much." she said in gulping sobs. "You don't want me anymore." With that said, she tried to crawl off the bed. She was past reasoning now, so he pulled her to him again, held on tight and rocked her—for a very long time.

When her sobbing finally subsided and she was whimpering quietly, he began talking to her. He didn't loosen his grip but just kept talking. He told her that he still found her as beautiful as the day they had met—the day he had fallen in love. He said, at first, seeing her bruises had made him feel so guilty and helpless that he didn't know what to do. He had never stopped wanting to make love to her, but she was in so much pain. Again, he didn't know what to do. "I'm so sorry, baby. I should have talked to you about it. I love you and need you as much as I ever have. Maybe even more because when I came in to see you lying unconscious on the floor, I didn't even know if you were alive. And I'm so goddamned happy that you are here with me. I have really fucked this up. I am so sorry, baby." He continued rocking her. "Can you forgive me?"

"But do you want me? Just like this? With bruises and swollen eyes and snot all over my face?"

Cade yanked his t-shirt over his head, wiped her face and pushed her damp hair back. "I love you, Lydia, just like you are now. I will never stop loving you." He nuzzled her next and nipped at her collarbone. Then he moved his mouth to suckle first one breast then the other. Neither of them would ever forget the way they came together so explosively that night. Both of them knew that real healing had begun and that their love was powerful.

Chapter 20

The next morning, Lydia woke up smiling. Cade still loved her and they had made passionate love last night. And he was here, lying on his back sleeping next to her. She propped herself up next to him and began to trace patterns in the dark hair covering his chest. She was making letters and concentrating so hard that she squealed when he grabbed her hand, rolled her over and entered her with one powerful thrust that seemed urgent. As he moved within her, she felt the contractions of an orgasm washing over her with more speed and intensity than ever before. In just a few minutes, they both lay panting in each other's arms.

"God, baby! You make me wild."

She leaned up to kiss his chin and smiled at him, but he looked at the clock. "Baby, I've got to get some work done today. How about we come back to play later?"

"Oh, Cade, just stay a little longer," she said as she stretched luxuriously and spread her legs. "Please?"

He stayed.

At some point, Lydia fell back asleep and when she woke

up, he was gone. She got out of bed and, after showering, realized that she felt much better today. She thought the pain in her face was definitely receding. Maybe she wouldn't need her pain pills. She needed to get back to real life—some kind of schedule—some kind of purpose. She would go talk to Cade right now about it. She made her way to the kitchen where she smelled coffee.

He was on the phone but cut it short when Lydia padded into the room. She threw her arms around his waist and pressed her body up against his. He gave her a gentle kiss on the top of her head and put her away from him. "Have you had pain pills this morning?"

She stomped her foot and said with huff, "Cade, I'm so much better today. I don't want to take any more pain pills. They make me feel slurry."

He laughed. "I'm not sure that's a word, but I get what you mean. We'll see how the day goes." Then he picked her up and sat her on the counter.

She squirmed to get down, "Oh no, you don't! I am not in the mood for one of your serious 'counter talks'!"

But he held her fast. "Just hold on, little girl. You may feel better, but there's still a lot of work to do. Connor has called Rory down from Wausau to help us so I can stay with you more. There's nothing you need to do but rest. Besides, there are still a few reporters out there so you're not going anywhere." Lydia looked unconvinced so he continued, "You know I do think you might be well enough for me to spank your bottom, so don't push me. Got it?"

She pouted but said, "Got it."

"Good, I need you to pay attention." Cade looked so stern that Lydia was nervous. "The senator wasted no time 'leaking' his story to the press. You know that he blames everyone but himself. He has made it look like you came on to him, I was the jealous husband, and Connor a wild man who has caused him grievous injury."

This news enraged Lydia, but she could see that Cade was working hard to control his anger and she didn't want to make things more difficult for him. She gulped, let out a big sigh and put her hands on his chest while tears she could not control filled her eyes. She turned her head so he wouldn't see, but he brought her head gently to his chest and let her cry.

They both struggled with their emotions for several long moments. Then he continued. "There's nothing we can do about this for the time being and we have the best people working on it. Also, you are safe. These are the things I want you to think about it. Okay, baby?" Lydia nodded as he lifted her down with instructions to sit at the table.

Cade made her some breakfast and then they talked about next steps. An hour later, they had a plan—at least for the immediate future. Because they didn't know how much time the case involving the senator would take—going to trial would drag it all out—they decided on a temporary schedule. Cade would do all the work he could from home and the security detail would continue until there was no danger. Cade had talked with Lydia's boss in the school-to-work program as well as her principal at the early childhood center. They decided that working on the grant while teaching early childhood for this summer would be too much so they would speak to Lydia later this week to see what she wanted to do. Sarah could pick up Lydia's slack this summer in either place, and she would also come every day to keep her company. Cade then revealed to Lydia that he had called her father and brother and Lola as well, to let them know she was safe and healing and that what they were hearing was not the truth.

Again, Lydia was teary. "Oh, I'm so sorry, Cade, but I was thinking about how hard it would be for me to call my family.

I was thinking that my father might actually believe the senator and Lola—oh, I miss her so much—she would be so upset to, well, to see my face. Thank you so much for calling them."

"You know, I don't know about your dad. He was very concerned and is anxious to talk to you. And your sister seemed to understand you would call her when you felt better. You can do that whenever you are up to it."

Again, she threw her arms around his neck and kissed him lightly on his neck and jaw. "I love you so much, Cade!"

"I'm glad because I need to get to work and you are either going back to bed or settling in on the couch. Which is it?"

"Aargh! I'm going to die of boredom!"

"Well, there is one more choice," Cade said as he covered her bottom with his hand. "Are you interested in that one? It's looking more and more interesting to me."

Lydia turned, made her way to the couch and picked up a book. She looked sullenly up at him, "Are you happy?"

He laughed and went into his office to work.

She was dozing on and off in her cozy little couch nest when her phone rang with a number she did not recognize. When she picked up, the caller disconnected. This happened a couple more times in the next fifteen minutes. Finally, Lydia tried calling the number back. She was thinking it might be a reporter and she wanted to give them a piece of her mind. But the voice on the other end was a woman—a young woman. She sounded anxious. Lydia tried to be kind. "This is Lydia McCauley. I see that you have been calling me. Can I help you?"

There was a pause and then a quavering voice said, "I've

been afraid to call you and I can't tell you who I am, but there is something you need to know."

Lydia didn't want to lose her so she just said, "I understand."

"What happened to you with the senator—it also happened to me. I mean, I understand the story the senator has put out there is not true so I *think* the same thing happened to you."

Lydia thought fast and asked, "I'm glad you called. It must have been difficult. Why do you want to tell me this?"

"So you know you are not alone and…"

Lydia waited.

"And because I want the senator exposed. You and I are not the only ones. I know someone else."

Lydia couldn't help but say, "My God!" Then she paused and asked, "Do you want to talk in person?"

"I do," the woman said tensely, "but it would have to be a secret. I am so afraid of the senator. He has so much power. He can ruin lives. My life has never been the same since he… attacked me. He knows how to wreck lives."

Lydia made a snap decision and said, "I believe what you're saying is true and I will meet with you whenever and wherever you want, but I have to bring my friend Sarah. You understand I could not come alone."

"Yes. And I will bring my friend who was also accosted by the senator. Do you know where Cave Point Beach is, near Devil's Lake? It's secluded there. I can be there tomorrow at 2:00 pm. Can you meet me?"

Lydia understood that if there were other women the senator had snared who were willing to go public, it would make the case against him very strong. They might even be able to bring him down. So even though she knew Cade could absolutely know nothing of this, she had to go. Sarah would be more than willing to come along.

"You were very brave to call me. I can't tell you how much this means to me. You know what I look like from the media so you find me. I will be there tomorrow. And thank you so much!"

Lydia called Sarah and asked her to drive out to their house *now*!

Chapter 21

"Sarah is coming out to keep me company for a while. She's going to stop and get some burgers and a shake for me. Do you want some lunch?" Lydia stood in the doorway to Cade's office and fought to sound casual when she was so excited to tell Sarah about the caller and nervous about how to pull off going out with Sarah.

Sarah came with bags full of Cade's favorite burgers and fries and a couple of milkshakes. He took a break and ate with the girls, then announced that he would be holed up for the afternoon but Lydia should let him know if she needed anything.

As soon as Cade left the room, Lydia led Sarah down the long hall to the master bedroom.

Sarah had only seen that room once when Lydia was recovering but hadn't paid much attention. She was impressed now that she had the chance to look around. "That's a fucking huge bed, Lydia, my God! Everything in here is goddamn gigantic."

Lydia giggled. Sarah frequently used language that Cade would never allow and she wasn't sure Connor would either, but then Sarah was so independent. Lydia admired it but did not aspire to it. The mildly Dominant/submissive dynamic she had with Cade suited her perfectly. She grabbed Sarah's hand and dragged her over to the sitting area. "I've got something big to tell you, Sarah," she whispered.

"Okay, but why are you whispering?"

"Because Cade will be crazy if he finds out anything about this. That's why I need your help."

"I'm in," said Sarah. "Spill!"

Lydia told Sarah all about the call from the "mystery woman" who had also been accosted by the senator and what it could mean. Then she told her about the meeting she had arranged which would require Sarah to come along."

"But how are we going to get out of here?" Sarah asked. "Cade watches over you like a hawk."

"Yes, it will be hard, maybe even impossible, but I have to try. If he finds out, he could do something so scare this woman off and I just can't let that happen. I am willing to suffer the consequences if he finds out."

"Wow!" said Sarah. "I know what kind of consequences Cade gives out but I agree, there is no other way. You know, I think Connor will have some consequences for me too if we get caught."

"Yes, he might. You don't have to come with me. I can do it alone."

"I could never live with myself if I let you go alone. Let's figure out a plan. We have to do this!"

It turned out to be a little easier to get away the next day than Lydia had originally thought. Cade had been working nonstop. He was constantly on the phone with Connor and Rory, and when he wasn't on the phone, he was working at his drafting table. When Sarah showed up for lunch again, Cade seemed happy to have her there to distract Lydia. He ate quickly and was heading back to his office when she reminded him that she had her last check up with the doctor at 1:00 on Wednesday afternoon. She could tell by his look that he had forgotten. Sarah saw her opportunity.

"Cade, maybe I could take Lydia to the checkup. It will take a couple of hours with drive time. If I take her, you don't have to interrupt your work."

Lydia had barely been out of the house since the attack, even with Cade, so the idea of her going with Sarah made him anxious. But the reporters had disappeared and Lydia's face, though still bruised, was healing well. He looked at Sarah, clearly considering the possibility.

Lydia held her breath.

"I suppose it would be safe for the two of you to go," he said warily. "However, I don't want you to go anywhere else. Go and come right back. Call me when you are leaving to come home. And keep your phone on. Understand?"

They both agreed quickly before he changed his mind. They were pulling out of the driveway by noon and headed for Cave Point Beach at Devil's Lake. They were quiet for a long time, and then Sarah asked, "Lydia, are you nervous about this meeting? I mean, you don't know these women. Maybe it's some kind of trap."

"I'm a little on edge, but I don't think there is any kind of trap. Sarah, when this woman called me, she sounded so afraid and maybe even a little desperate. I think it can only be a good thing for us to share our stories, even if we can't use them to put down the senator."

Lydia's sincere words struck Sarah. Lydia was such a good and kind person. She always put the welfare of others first. It seemed so unfair that she had experienced such emotional and physical trauma at the hands of that evil man. Sarah could feel her rage bubbling up. "You're right, Lydia. We are doing the right thing. And besides, I brought some protection along."

She reached into her purse and brought out a handgun.

"Oh my God, Sarah! Where did you get that? Do you know how to use it? You can't bring that out!"

"Don't worry. I do know how to use it. My brother gave it to me when I got my own apartment and showed me how to use it. It's been a while but I remember. And of course, I won't bring it out unless we end up in some danger. You brought me along for safety, right?"

"I asked you along because you are my friend and I need you. Please put that gun away."

As they entered the state park, Lydia's phone rang. It was the mystery woman. She explained exactly where they were and how to get there. As they talked, Lydia could see a young woman standing next to a blue mini-Cooper. Lydia waved. The woman who waved back was probably in her late twenties. She had long red hair and was quite beautiful. It made her sick to think of the senator preying on this young woman. She stood alone so Lydia asked Sarah to stay in the car as they met.

Even though Lydia was now a bit nervous, she had come this far and this meeting could be so important. She smiled and approached the girl. "My name is Lydia. I want to thank you again for calling me."

The young woman got tears in her eyes and said, "Did he do that to you?"

Lydia forgot how her face looked and understood how disconcerting it must be. "He did. But really, I am healing well now. I am okay."

The young woman introduced herself as Tracy and as she reached out to hug Lydia, she said, "I'm so glad you came. And I'm so sorry you were hurt. Maybe if I had been brave enough to come out with my story sooner, this would never have happened to you." She was ready to cry but gathered herself. "Seeing you makes everything clear now. We *have* to go after Senator Jacobi. No matter the consequences."

Lydia agreed and they hugged again.

At that point, Sarah could wait no longer and got out of the car, and Tracy signaled two other young women in her car to join them. Tracy's friends were Emily and Coco. Coco was hearing-impaired, so the girls began to sign as well as talk to each other.

Chapter 22

The day was getting warm so they found a place to sit in the shade and each young woman told her traumatic story of being "used" by the senator. One of the most shocking things that Lydia learned from Tracy was that Jennifer Hyde did not work for the Special Services Office.

"Did you notice that you were never taken to her office but always the senator's. We think the senator pays her to recruit young women for sex."

"Wow! Senator Jacobi put a lot of work, planning and money into procuring young women. He also is really good at hiding things, covering his tracks and using his position to get people to believe him. It's hard to believe there are people like him at the capitol."

Each young woman continued, and by the time they each told their sadly similar stories, they were all crying. In the group, Coco, the one who was hearing-impaired, had been the first victim. The senator must have thought she would be easy because she couldn't hear or talk. Lydia could only think of her sister Lola being taken advantage of because of her handicap, so she was most upset by Coco's story. However, each story held its own horrors. When Lydia finished her story, they were all quietly crying and no one said anything for a while.

Then Sarah spoke up. "I am so moved by all of your stories. You are all so brave, and I can't believe the courage you all possess. I think, together, you can do this. You can ruin the senator. What do you think is your next move?"

Lydia's first thought was that they should all meet with the lawyer Cade's friend Anson had suggested. He had experience with sexual assault cases.

Emily, who was a pre-law student, pointed out that getting convictions in sexual assault cases, and even rape, through the court system was still very difficult for most women even after the 'Me Too' movement, unless the women were rich and famous. The burden of proof is on the victim. The senator's knowledge, money and power had protected him so far. Emily thought it would be better to contact a journalist—a woman journalist who had broken stories like this before. There were a couple of well-known ones in Madison.

Tracy pointed out that all of this was dangerous for them. Yes, it was helpful to have all four of them come forward, but the backlash was likely to be intense. "There are those who simply don't believe women—ever. And then there are the supporters of Senator Jacobi who may see it as political and will threaten us or come after us. On top of that, my husband will have an absolute fit if he finds out I even met with you this afternoon. What will your husband say, Lydia?"

Lydia just shook her head and Sarah spoke up. "You know Cade's head will explode when he finds out where we have been today. Connor's too. This is such a difficult decision!"

The other two women weren't married but had significant others who would certainly not be happy. They were quiet for a few moments.

Then Tracy addressed all the women, "I have been afraid

to come out with my story for such a long time, but I know I can't live with myself if I don't. The men in our lives may love us but they just don't understand. We have to do this quickly before they stop us. The decision really comes down to the police/lawyer/justice system or the media. Time is of the essence. We have to decide now—today."

The women made a pros and con chart, argued, cried, and finally, after more than an hour, decided they would call Anita Black who was a well-known journalist and advocate for women's rights. She had done the big exposé on the CEO of Holman Corporation, a couple of years ago. The man had gone to prison, after his stocks lost half their worth. Hopefully she could bring down the senator. Tracy had Anita Black's number so she called her and told her that she had a story for her about sexual assault, but she would have to meet with a group of women now—and they would not come to her office. She would have to meet them. Anita enthusiastically agreed and told them to meet her in the back room of a coffee shop on the west side. She would be there in twenty minutes.

Tracy looked at all the women. "I don't know if you feel the same—and it's okay if you don't—but I have to do this."

"Me too," they all agreed.

Coco signed, "Take courage!"

Later, they would remember Coco's sign as a motto that kept them going.

Chapter 23

By the time they had arranged to secretly meet journalist Anita Brown, it was 4:00. Cade would expect Lydia and Sarah to be home soon. They still needed a couple of hours of freedom so they had to extend the ruse they had already set up to get away. Lydia had an idea. She called Cade.

"Hi, Cade. I'm done at the doctor's and he is happy with the healing."

"Great, baby! Where are you now?"

"Well, that's why I called. We ran into a couple of friends from the school-to-work program. It's so nice to see them and we thought it would be fun to grab a bite to eat and catch up. Can I do that?"

There was a pause. "You know I wanted you two to come straight home."

"I know and we were walking to the car and ran into them. Oh, Cade, it's so nice to see friends again. And we'll just go to a quiet little place near here. Please, Cade! We'll be careful and I'll call you when we leave to come home. Please let me stay."

"All right. But you are pushing things here, little girl. If you are not home before 7:00, there will be hell to pay. Got it?"

"Yes, Cade, I got it. Thank you, I love you. See you later."

Lydia breathed a huge sigh of relief as she hung up, then Sarah called Connor. The girls thought it best to then turn off their phones.

Anita Brown was a very attractive, tall, professional-looking woman of about thirty-five. She had her white-blonde hair pulled back in a tight ponytail. There was a noticeable sophistication about her that exuded intelligence and poise. She met them in the front room of Serendipity Coffee and Tea, shook hands with each of the women and said, "I am honored to meet you brave women. Let's go in the back where we can talk."

Anita first told them about herself. She had been a journalist for fifteen years in Chicago and then Madison. She was especially interested in women's issues and had therefore worked on a couple of high-profile sexual assault stories. She said that in both cases, her story was instrumental in bringing the perpetrator down. She was proud of that, as the justice system still put barriers in the way of women victims.

Tracy interrupted her to ask some questions about the timeline, their privacy and the possibilities of backlash from the public and/or the senator. Anita told her that those were excellent questions. She thought the first part of the story could come out quite soon—within the week, in the largest Madison newspaper. She thought it might be released in at least a couple of parts but would have to hear the stories first. Anita explained that she would not use their names, but that didn't mean that their identities would remain secret. She also said she knew of the senator and men like him were ruthless. He could make things unpleasant for them for a while. Still, she said, she believed that if they went forward, he would be brought down and the chances of them being vindicated were higher than going through the traditional justice system. Anita wondered if they were aware that Senator Jacobi had already beaten assault charges twice.

This was a lot of disturbing information to process and the women were silent. Anita asked, "I know this is a lot. Does anyone want to tell me what you are thinking?"

Lydia said, "Listening to you, makes me more sure than before that this is the way to go. However, I know that it will be almost impossible to talk my husband into this. You can see that I still have bruises inflicted by the senator and my husband's protectiveness is on a high level. I am really set on doing this, but I am not sure of the best way to approach him."

Anita was nodding while Lydia spoke. "I completely understand. I would love to hear your stories today, but you are under no obligation to go ahead unless you decide that is what you want. I have, in the past, talked with boyfriends and husbands to help them understand the value of using the media. Usually, I am able to win them over, but not every time. I would be willing to meet with those who care about you to explain things if you think that would help."

Lydia and Sarah knew they would need Anita's help in convincing their men and that it would be very difficult. Lydia had a feeling they were both probably in big trouble for what they did today. But she was committed.

Over the next hour, all four women told their stories, beginning with Coco, using Tracy as an interpreter, and ending with Lydia, whose face still showed signs of the senator's abuse. Even the normally cool and collected Anita Brown was in tears by the time they were done. She assured them that theirs were the most important stories she would ever tell and hoped they would move forward.

They talked about arranging a meeting together with Anita and all of their partners. Sarah spoke up and said that perhaps it would work out best to use Connor's house. She was not a victim so not on anyone's radar and his house was large and in the country. They tentatively set the meeting for Thursday evening. If there were those who could not make it, they should let Sarah know. The women exchanged contact information and, amid hugs and a few more tears, parted ways.

Chapter 24

Sarah texted Connor that they were on their way home. Then she again turned her phone off. The girls were uncharacteristically silent as they set out for home. Not only was there a lot to process after meeting and hearing the stories of three other sexual assault victims, but they were also now thinking about facing Cade and Connor to tell them the truth about what they had been doing today. Lydia considered that she had defied Cade and lied to him—a few times over. He would think she had also put herself in danger. She was pretty sure she had never committed all of those sins together in one day before and she truly had a hard time imagining the depth of his wrath. On top of that, she had dragged Sarah along, getting her in trouble too. This was going to be unpleasant at best.

Sarah looked over at Lydia and saw that she was worried. Her friend had been through so much in the last week. Still, she knew that Cade was going to be furious. The idea that other women were ready to speak up about the senator would matter to him, but that would not have him excuse her behavior today.

"Lydia, I know you are having a hard time facing Cade and telling him the truth. But do you believe you did the right thing? I do. The testimonials from the four of you will turn the public irreversibly against the senator. Keep that in mind when Cade... well, when Cade..."

"Is paddling me relentlessly?"

Sarah reached over and patted Lydia's hand. "Maybe it won't come to that."

Lydia snorted, "You know it will! But you're right. I believe in this." Then she squeezed Sarah's hand and said, "I am afraid you are going to get it too, and I am sorry for that. You've been such a good friend."

"I'll be okay," Sarah said as they pulled into the long driveway leading to Cade's house. Suddenly, Sarah braked and they looked up to see their men standing in front of the garage with their arms folded over their chests and their faces angrier than either of the girls had ever seen.

Almost before the car stopped, both men moved in tandem to open the car doors nearest their respective women and pull them out none too gently. Taking hold of their upper arms, Lydia and Sarah found themselves begin dragged into the house. Wisely, neither of them said anything. The men also said nothing—yet.

Once inside, Cade made his way with Lydia to their bedroom and Connor directed Sarah to the bedroom on the lower level. This looked bad. And it was.

Cade sat down on the corner of their huge bed and drew Lydia to stand between his legs. He put his thumbs into her waistband and yanked her jeans and panties down past her knees. Then he grabbed her wrists so she was trapped.

"You defied me, lied to me, and did something dangerous. Right?"

Lydia nodded, knowing this was not the time for a full

explanation because he would not listen. And what he said was true.

"I think you knew how I would react and you did it anyway. Right?

Lydia nodded miserably, tears already forming in her eyes. For just a moment, Cade felt unsure of himself but when he thought about how anxious he was when, after Lydia had called to say she had met friends, the doctor's office called to ask if Lydia wanted to reschedule the appointment she had missed. When he realized she had not been to the doctor at all and that her phone was off, he knew she had lied to him. He had been angry and frantic. Connor was wildly angry with Sarah too. After they got the text that the girls were on their way home, the men decided their girls were going to get immediate and memorable spankings the minute they got home. There would be time for explanations and apologies later.

Now, with his nervous, tearful and bare-bottomed girl trapped between his legs, he decided to get on with it. Cade pushed her over one of his muscular thighs and held both of her legs with his other leg. He pulled her up tightly to him so that one arm was held against him, and the other he secured in the small of her back.

Lydia was crying now before he had even begun. The first smack took her breath away. Sometimes Cade began with a "warm up" but Lydia knew this would not be one of those times. The next smacks came down, over and over, in a steady rhythm sometimes spanking in the same spot two or three times which was nearly unbearable. Cade nearly always lectured Lydia while he was spanking, but this time he spanked silently and unyieldingly, and when he moved down to redden her thighs, she screamed. Her entire bottom was on fire, and now he was igniting her sensitive thighs. Normally, Lydia would have been screaming apologies and promising to be good forever. But not this time. As much pain as he was inflicting, Lydia would not beg forgiveness because she believed in her heart that she had done what she needed to do. This shocked Cade and he wasn't really sure what to do. Lydia's bottom was cherry red and quite swollen now yet she made no attempt to beg him to stop. He paused, resting his hot hand on her red-hot bottom.

"Have I made my point, Lydia? When you defy me and lie to me, you will find yourself getting spanked into next week every time! Do you understand me?"

Lydia caught her breath enough to say, "Yes, Cade, I understand, and I'm sorry I scared you. Please stop, Cade! It hurts so much!"

It was not lost on Cade that she did not say she was sorry for putting herself in danger and lying to him. He considered grabbing her hairbrush and adding some welts to her stubborn backside until she did, when she cried piteously, "Please, Cade, I know I defied you and lied to you and… and… I knew you would spank me. But I had to do it! Please stop and listen to me. Oh please, Cade!"

His heart melted and he pulled her up to his lap. He grabbed the bottom of his t-shirt to mop up her tears and brought her face into his neck. "God, Lydia! Don't you see? Your face is still bruised from the ordeal we went through a week ago. I worry about you every minute. And then you think it's okay to lie to me and sneak off? Do you have any idea how wild I was?"

"I do, Cade. I do understand. And I am so sorry I had to make you worry. But I didn't see any other way. Really! Please let me tell you what happened."

He rubbed her back and said, "Sure, baby. Drink some water and change into something that won't hurt that red bottom."

"Okay, but both of us—Sarah and I—need to talk to the two of you together."

Cade nodded. "Okay. Come out to the kitchen when you are ready."

Chapter 25

Sarah had anticipated Connor being angry enough to spank her—he had done it before—but knowing he was not as intense as Cade, she thought it might not be that bad. She had not counted on the fact that after Lydia's attack, both brothers were on high alert and in almost unmanageable protective mode. This made Connor hell-bent on teaching Sarah a lesson she would not forget.

Connor wanted to see if he could elicit compliance from his usually independent girl. He noticed she was quieter and more cooperative with the prospect of punishment than she had been in the past so when they reached the back bedroom downstairs, he led her to an empty corner and told her she was going to stand there and think about what she had done and about the hard spanking she was about to get. She looked at him wide-eyed, biting her lip, but moved with him as he took her arm to deposit her in the corner.

"Pull your pants and panties down, Sarah. Having a bare bottom will help you think better." Slowly, she followed his instructions. He was amazed that she did what she was told. "Good girl," he said as he took her arms and arranged them in back of her so her forearms rested just above the swell of her bottom. "Now, nose in the corner." When she didn't move, he gave her bare backside a mighty smack and barked, "Now!" She complied.

Connor had to admit that seeing his girl with his handprint on her bare bottom waiting in the corner for a spanking had him aroused. "Do some thinking, naughty girl, and I'll be back. If you move from there or even think about rubbing that bottom, I will know and it will go worse for you."

Sarah was mortified! She couldn't believe he would do this to her, and what she could believe even less was that she was obeying him. It was difficult not to move as the position was uncomfortable, but she tried. Sarah understood why Connor was angry. She had snuck around behind his back and lied to him. In her family, growing up, that would certainly have earned her a spanking. And it did on many occasions. She understood that Connor felt the need to teach her a lesson and that he did not want this repeated. He wanted her to think upon this unpleasant experience before considering doing anything like it again. But she couldn't help but feel a little sorry for herself so, though she fought it, tears began to appear on her cheeks. By the time he returned, she was sobbing quietly.

Connor did not plan to leave her long and actually spent the time pacing back and forth in the large, lower family room. He had already exposed her to something new—corner time. He knew she would hate it, but he really wanted to make an impression on her with this spanking. He had an idea and began rummaging around in the drawers and cupboards in the storage area adjacent to the family room. When he found what he was looking for, he went back to the bedroom to find Sarah obediently standing with nose still in the corner. He sat on the edge of the bed and said gruffly, "Come here."

Sarah turned to him and saw that he was holding a small

paddle. She couldn't help but gasp. He repeated, "Come here,"

She shuffled over as well as she could with her pants and panties around her knees, hobbling, and stood in front of him. Connor wasted no time in flipping her over one knee and began to spank her with his hand that was large enough to cover her entire bottom. Almost immediately, she began to beg him to stop.

"A spanking stops when I say so, little girl, and we have a ways to go!" He continued spanking, moving down to her sit spots and thighs. He planned that she would remember this spanking for a long while. "I plan to keep spanking you until this bottom is bright red. This is for sneaking around behind my back. Don't you ever do that again! Do you understand?"

"Yes, Connor, but please, please, it hurts so much!"

He stopped momentarily then and said, "I'll bet it does. It's supposed to! And if you hadn't lied to me too, this would be over now, but you did, so you're getting some of the paddle too!"

"Oh, Connor, no! Please! I can't stand it!"

Connor grabbed the paddle, and he didn't plan to use it long; he knew that the implement was much more painful than his hand. But he wanted this punishment to be remembered. The first smack brought a howl from Sarah that she kept up until she ran out of breath. After about twenty smacks, he could see he had raised a few welts that must hurt like hell so he stopped. Sarah was limp over his lap, her shiny, hot bottom now decorated with some deep red marks. It was a truly punished bottom and Connor was satisfied she would remember it.

Sarah tried to get up but he held her there, and though he gently rubbed her back, he said, "You stay right there for a while, little girl. I won't spank anymore, but I want you to think about how you look with your naughty red bottom up over my knee with some very red paddle marks and your panties at your knees. That's the picture I want in your head when you even think about doing anything like you did today. Got it?"

The picture he painted was memorable and painful. And though she still thought she and Lydia did what they had to, she really hoped she could avoid ever getting this kind of punishment again. "Got it," she answered as her sobs let up.

He let her up then pulled up her pants to a hiss that was satisfying to him.

"All right, let's go upstairs. I think Cade and I are ready to listen to your story now."

Twenty minutes later, Lydia and Sarah were sitting contritely, although a little uncomfortably, on the couch with Cade and Connor sitting across from them listening to their story. Both of the girls were still red-eyed and hiccupping. It was clear that Sarah had been subjected to Connor's anger in the same way as Lydia, but together, they got through the entire amazing story of their meeting with other victims and their commitment to telling their story to the public through Anita Brown.

Cade and Connor were dumbfounded. They listened without interrupting, but then had tons of questions and deep concerns.

The girls listened and then Sarah said, "We know you don't like this and have a million questions, which is why we arranged for... we thought maybe..."

Lydia continued, "We asked the other women to meet with us tomorrow, with Anita Brown *and* with all of our partners, so together we could explain everything to you. And, Connor, we sort of said, well, we sort of invited them to your house."

"What the hell?" Connor raged.

"Wait, before you get mad," interrupted Sarah. "Reporters

keep an eye on this place and your house is a little more isolated. Don't you think it's safer?"

Connor had to agree she was right, and though they were not at all sold on the idea of using the media instead of the court system to bring the senator to justice, in the end, they agreed to the meeting.

Finally, Sarah went to Connor, stood in his arms and said, "I understand your misgivings about this whole thing. I felt that way too. Until I saw Coco using sign language to tell her story about the abuse the senator had inflicted on her. Of course, I am enraged over what happened to Lydia, but now with Coco and the others, it just seems like we have no choice."

Connor took Sarah's face in his hands and kissed her forehead. "I get it, little girl, let's go home."

Chapter 26

The next night, Lydia and Cade went to Connor's about an hour before the scheduled meeting, to make sure there was at least something to snack on and drink for the group that would number eleven with all couples, Anita and, of course, Anson. It was a beautiful June evening and Connor opened the patio doors to let a gentle breeze overtake the room. They had just about everything set when Anita rang the doorbell. They went to answer it together and were surprised to find that Jackson Graves was there with her.

Connor welcomed them, and Sarah, who was always apt to name the elephant in the room, said to Anita, "I don't understand! Why is Jackson here? I thought we were going to be talking about not using the justice system to go after Senator Jacobi, but you've brought a lawyer with you?"

Anita and Jackson both smiled. Anita explained, "You're right, it does seem counterintuitive to have invited part of the court system into our discussion, but please trust me. Jackson is on our side and can help us." She paused then, looked up at him, and added, "Besides, he is my fiancé."

Before there could be any more discussion on that matter, the other women began to arrive with their partners. Tracy was married to Rob who, as it turned out, went to school with Connor; Emily brought her boyfriend Frank; and Coco was accompanied by her significant other, Janey, who also appeared to be her interpreter. Anson arrived soon after. Introductions were made all around, and Connor and Sarah made sure everyone had what they needed. Connor's great room easily accommodated all of them as they made themselves comfortable. Anita and Jackson stood so that everyone could see and hear them.

Anita began, "I want you to know how happy I am to see you all here tonight. No matter what happens, you women are some of the bravest I have ever met. Truly, your courage is commendable and it's an honor to know you. I hope I will be able to serve you. " She smiled sincerely, making eye contact with each one and continued. "What I want to do tonight is lay out the options you have, in an attempt to make the senator accountable. The choices are difficult and none of this is easy. First of all, going after sexual assault perpetrators is not a victim-friendly process. It is an institution-protection process. And that is especially true when politicians are concerned. Unless the senator is charged, convicted and found guilty in a court of law, he will not pay the price. The only real recourse for his victims is to wait until the next election to see if he will be voted out. Not only is this a mind-numbingly long process but it is so often unsuccessful—this is why. There's a mandatory mediation policy that was put forth by an act in 1995 that requires survivors to go through mediation as part of the complaint process before they can even file lawsuits. It takes forever."

Anita could see that the group had a hard time taking this in. It was time to let Jackson step up. He continued for her, "Women are generally afraid to come forward. It's nothing short of amazing that this group is considering it. The senator has no scruples and has used his influence to ruin the reputation of his accusers and even go after their families. In the two times he has been publicly accused before, he has used his own wealth to hire a team of lawyers who are experienced in saving and protecting men of wealth and power from harassment accusations."

Frustrated, Cade wiped his hand over his face and said, "Are you saying that even with the testimony of these four women, the chances that the senator will be held accountable are slim?

"Yes. That's what I am saying," said Jackson.

"But you think that if he is exposed in the media, there is more of a chance he will be taken down?" It was Connor who spoke up this time.

Again, Jackson replied, "Yes."

Now Tracy's husband Rob asked, "But can't he counterattack after it comes out and hurt us in the meantime?"

Anita responded, "None of these women will be named but, yes, he could go ahead and name those he knows, most likely Lydia, as she is the most recent." She paused while the men grumbled then went on. "Look. I understand that it's a frightening proposition. There *is* one more option. Let it go. Let him off scot-free, again."

Lydia suddenly stood. "No! No! I will not accept that option. I have to do what I can to bring him down. He can't keep doing this to women." She looked at Cade imploringly. "Please, Cade. Please say we won't let him get off!"

Cade, who was sitting on the floor with his arms resting on his knees, reached up to grab Lydia's hand to pull her down so she was sitting between his legs. He gently moved his hands up and down her arms and said, "Let's let Anita and Jackson continue, baby."

Anita spoke next. "This is all entirely up to you, all of you or any of you. Let me tell you how I'm thinking of doing this. Because the senator was using the Office of Special Services to recruit ASL interpreters and women who are hearing-impaired, it is a most egregious act. In general, the public does not like politicians who are accused, but they do not always lose their jobs. But this case is different. When I met with these women and personally heard their stories, I realized that there has probably never been a more powerful case against any political perpetrator. I believe that if the public heard these stories, the senator's denials would not be believed and his chances of being charged and ejected from the State Senate would be high."

She let that soak in for a minute before going on. "So, I propose using the video production people at Madison Media, to produce a mini-documentary featuring our four brave women. And you are brave, no matter what you decide today. It would be scheduled for release the day after my initial article exposing the senator. We will not name you, and in the video, we will artfully disguise you. I would want to work on the video tomorrow and release it the next day. I think that twenty-four hours after the video release, we will know what the senator plans to do.

Coco's partner asked, "What do you think the senator will do?"

"Well, the best-case scenario is that he immediately resigns. Worst case is a blanket denial and counter accusations against all of you. In any case, Madison Media will work with the police and sheriff's office to procure security for all of your homes. Because the senator actually came into your home, Lydia, we don't put much beyond him."

The entire group was very quiet. Finally, Jackson spoke up and said, "I came along tonight to help Anita explain the difficulties in bringing a case against the senator. I wanted you to hear it from both sides. I sympathize with you that this is a very difficult decision but want you to know that Anita and I will support whatever you choose."

Then Anita added, "I know this is a lot to process and I hate to say it, but time is not on our side. The senator has hired a well-known team and may go after any of you in a proactive defense move. We would like to be ready to head that off. I'm going to find a space to wait while you talk about it. I would really like to leave tonight with your decision. And I will respect whatever that is." Jackson and Anita retreated to the far reaches of the lower level to let the group work toward agreement.

Chapter 27

At the onset, Emily's partner Frank was the most vocal against proceeding with the video to be used to expose Senator Jacobi. "I don't think I want Emily involved in this. I think all of you risk your own reputations by making these accusations," he said. "And I know I don't want my girl mixed up in this. Come on, Emily. I've heard enough. Let's go."

The room got very quiet as everyone watched to see how Emily would respond.

"I think I'll stay, Frank. You can leave if you want to. Someone here will bring me home," Emily responded, trying to sound casual even though she was upset.

"No. I want you to come with me now. We need to talk about this," Frank said as he took her arm to propel her toward the door.

Emily wrested her arm away and said, "This is not about you, Frank. I am staying to hear Anita out. As I said, if you want to go, go."

Now Frank looked angry. "We *are* going to discuss this

later. Don't make any commitments if you know what's good for you."

Emily's face turned red but she turned away from him and made a dismissive gesture with her arm. "Just go, Frank."

Frank looked around the room. "You're all going to be sorry about this. No one will believe you. I'm not sure I even believe you," he said as stomped out the door.

When the door slammed, Emily turned to the group and said, "I'm so sorry."

"There's no need for you to be sorry, Emily. In fact, Frank's reaction is an example of the viewpoint of many people when women come out against attackers. It's unfortunate but real. It's something all of us need to consider before we go forward," said Anita who had come back up to see who was shouting. "Are you okay?"

"Thank you. I'm fine. Really," she said with a sigh.

Lydia got up and went to sit next to Emily as the discussion resumed. Her reassuring smile diffused the situation and bolstered Emily's confidence.

Anson had watched Emily's boyfriend try to bully and disrespect her and admired the fact that she did not give in. It took some amount of control on his part not to step in and say something to the jerk, but she had handled it. As he watched Emily, he felt a sudden urge to protect her. She was a small, young woman, with strawberry-blonde hair that curled in wisps around her face but hung past her shoulders. Her large, hazel eyes and sprinkling of freckles made her appear young, but her lush lips and appealing curves were sexy. She really deserved better than that asshole, Frank.

Another hour of thoughtful, passionate, and exhausting discussion, with some anger and tears, finally allowed the group to come up with a decision and a plan. It was agreed that they all needed to do what it took to stop the senator from ever hurting anyone else.

The group also decided to take the offer of security provided for them for the duration of the case. They agreed not to go anywhere alone and to be diligent about schedules and awareness of things happening around them at all times. They decided together that what they were doing was the right thing, and that was enough motivation.

Anson spent some time taking statements from each of the women about their charges against Senator Jacobi. The statements were then officially on record and, in some cases, reminded the women of their stories, which would help them articulate them for the video and/or any occasions that would require them to relate what happened.

Anita's exposé would come out the day after next in the newspaper, both in print and online, and they hoped that the video would come out one day later. On-camera interviews were done the next day and the videographer had but two days to put it together into a meaningful piece. Now they waited.

Both Cade and Connor alternately cajoled and threatened the girls into absolutely following the rules. They were never to be out of their sight and, in fact, would accompany them to work when necessary. They were not to answer their phones and, for the time being, were not allowed to leave home without at least one of the men. It was a stressful time as they waited for the article to come out and for the reaction it created.

They did not have to wait long. Anita must have never slept because the article broke the next day on the Madison Media website. From then on, it was an explosion of news. The story of the four women coming forward to accuse the senator was out on all social media and all news outlets— digital and print. So far, the senator had not been "reached for comment," but waiting for the public reaction was nerve-wracking.

While they waited, the four-minute video was released. The videographer had done a masterful job of hiding the faces of the women and also of editing their interviews down to the most meaningful and poignant parts. The video coming on the heels of the article caused a sensation. The reaction was stunning! There was widespread condemnation of the senator and petitions were begun to remove him from office. It seemed to be going well. Until the third day.

The senator came out, fully denying it all and calling it a political hoax. But the worst thing was that he named Lydia McCauley as a liar, telling the world that she had come on to him because she was unhappy in her marriage. He claimed to have been attacked at Lydia's home after she had invited him there.

Even though they had been told to expect this, Lydia had not imagined how hard it would be on her or on Cade. He was working hard to contain his rage and Connor was not much help. The reporters soon amassed on the road at the end of their driveway, and they were once again prisoners in their home. Anson arranged for the police and sheriff departments to disperse the reporters, but all of them were anxious about what would happen next. They decided to turn off all devices and watch nothing on television but old movies. Connor and Sarah stayed over and all of them had quite a sleepless night.

Just as it was getting light the next morning, Cade heard what he thought was a pounding on their front door and the doorbell ringing incessantly. He grabbed his gun, telling Lydia not to move from that bed! He called out to Connor and Sarah to stay in their room while he checked it out. He turned the porch camera to view and saw that Anita and Jackson were frantically pounding on the door. He quickly let them in. "What the hell is going on? Are you okay? It's not even 6:00 am, is it?" he said as he yanked the door open.

Anita seemed out of breath, and they were both excited.

"Anita has something to tell you! Where is Lydia?" asked Jackson.

"I'm right here," said a sleepy Lydia. "What is it?"

"I thought I told you to stay in bed," Cade growled.

Lydia bit her lip as Connor and Sarah joined her.

"For God's sake! Tell us!" yelled Sarah.

"Yes! Yes!" said Anita. "Come over here. You'll want to be sitting for this news!" They all moved into the great room and Cade turned on the fireplace. Sarah had run to get Anita some water as she still seemed out of breath.

Cade was impatient. "Goddammit, Anita, tell us!" he commanded.

"Okay. Last night, I got a call from a woman who told me Senator Jacobi had tried to rape her in his office about five years ago."

"Oh my God!" said Lydia and Sarah in tandem.

"There's more! She asked if I would join her on a Zoom link in fifteen minutes, as she had something to show me. Well, of course, I did. She sent the link at exactly 10:00 pm and when I logged in, there on the screen were the faces of twelve women! The woman who had contacted me identified herself and told me that I was looking at twelve women who had been accosted by the senator who now wanted to come forward. They said they were so motivated by the four women who had the courage to speak out, they felt they could finally do the same and would I help them get their stories out?"

"I know this is important, but what does it mean, Anita? What will happen?" asked a stunned Lydia.

"I am going to meet with them, just like I did with you, at noon. Then I'll release another story and get the videographer. By tonight, the story will be out. But I haven't told you the best part. Jackson, you tell them."

"Well, I called Senator Jacobi's chief of staff last night at midnight and told him what was about to happen. Of course, he denied everything *but* we got a call just before we headed over here this morning that Senator Jacobi has called a news conference for later this morning where he reportedly will resign as State Senator!"

Sarah began jumping up and down. "We did it! We did it! I can't believe it! We did it!"

Lydia turned in Cade's arms where she had been nestled and smiled up at him. He took her face in his hands and said, "You did it, baby! I'm so proud of you," and kissed her like they were all alone.

Lydia and Sarah then turned their attention to Anita, who had worked so hard to make this happen. They went to hug her, but Jackson stopped them and said, "Just hang on a second!" as he pulled Anita into his arms for a kiss and said, "You did it, love! You pulled this off."

It was a happy but tired group of people sitting at the table while Cade and Lydia made breakfast. They decided to wait together to watch the senator's press conference later in the morning. But it never happened.

During the middle of the night, the senator, apparently finally facing the truth of his actions, tried to leave the country. His estranged wife actually alerted the police to the fact that he had emptied all of their accounts and had called her to say he would never see her again. The authorities apprehended him as he tried to board a plane for Brazil, and he was now being held for a hearing. Anson called and informed them all that there was no turning back for Senator Jacobi now. His career was over.

Chapter 28

The profound relief experienced by the brave group of women who exposed the senator was well earned. They and those who cared about them felt a keen sense of accomplishment, but they were exhausted. It had been a stressful ordeal for everyone involved.

None of the women were publicly named in Anita's writing or in the video, but because the attack on Lydia had been the most recent and her name was known, she was hounded by the media for interviews or statements. Cade still insisted that she never go anywhere without him and he had a million rules for her to follow. There were days when Lydia felt as if it wasn't really over at all, and she became cranky and unreasonable. Cade held on to his temper as long as he could, but one evening during an argument, when she threw a book at his head, her bottom paid the price and she found herself in the corner after a long, hard spanking. He threatened her with a naughty girl plug if she didn't get a grip, so she remained compliantly with her nose on the wall until he called her to him.

He really wanted to help her and wracked his brain for a

way they could take a break. He talked to Connor about it, who said, "Why don't you take her up to the cabin for a few days of peace and quiet. It would be a change of scene and you both might get some perspective on this whole thing."

Cade thought that was a great idea so he and Connor began making plans. They called their cousin Rory who had made the decision to move down to Madison to join their business. Though he wasn't planning on the final move until July 4th, he was going to make a few trips down to finalize his role in the company and look for a house. Cade told him that they needed him for a few days now so they could take a much-needed break, and he said he could come right away. Then Cade called Lydia's principal to see if Lydia could wait until the second session of summer school to begin teaching. That would be in mid-July. Her principal was also her friend and loved the idea of giving Lydia a break. She would make all the necessary arrangements.

The next morning, Cade was up at dawn, leaving Lydia to sleep in. By the time she woke up and made her way to the kitchen, Cade had begun loading supplies into the truck.

"What are you doing? Are you going somewhere? Hey, where are you taking my bike?"

Cade walked over to her and lifted her up so her legs were forced to go around his waist.

"I don't know what you're up to but this is nice," she said with a smile.

"Yeah. It's going to get a lot nicer. We are getting out of here! I thought you need some peace and we need some time alone together—so we're going up to the cabin for a few days. How does that sound?"

"Oh, Cade, that sounds wonderful!" She leaned in for a kiss and he didn't unlock until she was breathless. "But, Cade, what about your work? What about my work? Who will watch the house, what about—"

"Whoa, baby girl. I took care of everything, and I'll tell you about it on the way. Come on. Get yourself ready and pack. I want to get on the road as soon as possible."

Lydia looked up at him lovingly. "I don't deserve you, Cade McCauley."

He kissed her forehead, turned her around, gave her bottom a swat and said, "Hurry up!"

Lydia looked over her shoulder and pouted. "Do we have to go now, Cade? Right now?

He looked at her quizzically as she reached down to the hem of his t-shirt she had worn to bed and a pulled it over her head. There she stood, completely naked, with that mane of pitch-black hair trailing down her back to the swell of her bottom that featured his pink handprint. His cock went rock-hard and he growled as he reached out for her. She slipped away and ran down the hall with him in hot pursuit. They did not get on the road until almost noon, but they were both sated and smiling.

The June weather could not have been more perfect. Lydia and Cade did what they wanted, when they wanted. And what they mostly wanted was each other. The stress of the last two weeks had taken a toll on each of them emotionally, and until they were safely alone together, far from memories of Lydia's attack, they didn't realize what they had been missing. They made love everywhere—the beach, the lake, the hammock, which was a little challenging, the picnic table and once, late at night, out on the dock in the moonlight. Lydia could feel the peace seeping into her and Cade was delighted to see it.

On the fourth day of their idyllic time together, they sat together watching the fire in the outdoor fireplace, when Lydia said, "You know. I miss Connor and Sarah. They were so supportive during that whole nightmare and spent so much time caring for us." She was tracing a pattern on Cade's chest which he had come to know meant she was either going to tell him something he would not like or ask him something she was unsure of.

"What are you thinking, baby?"

She looked at him then. "Do you think we could ask them to come up here? I think it would be so much fun! Please?"

Cade didn't know if he was ready to give up his alone time, but Connor and Sarah seemed to have a relationship at least started and the four of them had grown closer over the last month.

"Sure. I'll call Connor and see when they can come."

Lydia stood up and clapped her hands. "Great! We can take out the pontoon and the jet ski, and tomorrow, let's go get ribs to put on the grill and—"

"Okay, okay, let's just see if they can make it. Let's go in and call them."

Chapter 29

Connor and Sarah had said they would be up there in time for dinner the next day, and Cade thought he had never seen Lydia so excited. She cleaned and cooked all day in sort of a frenzy. Finally, he picked her up and sat her on the counter to get her attention. "Baby, you've got to settle down. You're wearing me out! I'm going to pour you a glass of wine, and I want you to come and sit with me on the porch."

"But, Cade, I still have to—"

He interrupted, "All you have to do right now is mind me. Got it?"

Lydia was just feeling the mellow of the wine take effect when she heard the sound of a vehicle on the crunchy gravel driveway. Cade heard it too and was there when Lydia threw open the door to greet Connor and Sarah.

"Oh, I'm so glad you're here…" Suddenly, Lydia went silent as her jaw dropped open. Instead of Connor and Sarah, there stood Cade's cousin Rory and Lydia's twin sister Lola!

There was a moment of silence while Lydia realized who was there. "Oh my God, Lola!" was all she could say before she burst into tears and the girls embraced—for a long time. "How did you… What are you doing? Who brought… Lydia's hands flew in sign language to ask questions but she was so stunned, nothing came out complete. She looked back at Cade, who had tears in his eyes watching the twins in this surprise reunion. Lola stepped back to put her hand very gently up to Lydia's face where the bruises were fading but still visible. She began to sob and hugged Lydia again.

After a few moments, Rory stepped forward and put his arm around Lola to draw her back. "Lola has been so worried about you. I thought it would be good for her—well, for both of you—to be together, after all you've been through, Lydia. So, Cade had the idea that we should come up for a reunion for a couple of days and let Connor and Sarah hold down the fort and then join us this weekend."

Lydia turned her tear-stained face to Cade and threw her arms around his neck, sobbing, "Thank you! Thank you! Thank you!"

Lydia would look back on dinner that night at the cabin as one of the most special memories of her life. She was there with her wonderful husband, her beloved twin sister whom she had not seen since her wedding, and her sister's apparent love interest, who was also Cade's cousin. Her life, that had seemed so depressing just a few days ago, now seemed perfect. Cade watched his girl glow with happiness.

As the sun set, the men went out to build an outdoor fire and the sisters were left to clean up and talk together. Now that they were alone, Lydia asked Lola the question that had been uppermost in her mind since they arrived.

"How is it you are with Rory? What is going on? I see the way you look at each other," Lydia signed.

Lola explained that she and Rory had been attracted to each other at the wedding—really attracted. They had been "talking" almost every day since Lola went back to school.

They had a wonderful time together—Lola used the sign for 'magic' when she described it—and now she thought they were pretty serious. Lola turned to Lydia and signed, "I think we are falling in love!"

Lydia teared up again and hugged her sister. "I am so happy for you! But I don't know Rory. Tell me about him. Is he like Cade and Connor? Have you, well, have you slept with him?" she asked.

"I don't know if he is like Cade and Connor, but what we have works. And yes," she admitted, blushing, "I have slept with him."

By the time Cade came in to call the girls out to the fire, they were talking, signing and giggling like crazy. Cade noticed that they had also poured themselves big glasses of wine. He might have warned Lydia off that extra glass, but she was so thrilled to have her sister here, he couldn't scold her.

As they went to sit around the fire, Lola moved to sit rather intimately between Rory's legs. Lydia's eyes grew wide and she looked at Cade, who signaled her to stay quiet about it.

As they got comfortable, Cade asked the big question, "Rory, it looks like you and Lola know each other pretty well. What's been going on?"

Rory and Lola's eye met. She nodded, and Rory began telling the story of how they had been attracted to each other at first sight when they met at Lydia and Cade's rehearsal dinner. After the wedding when they went back to their respective homes in Wausau and out in DC, they began to communicate in long conversations, using iPad screens and using the phone for texting.

Rory looked at Lydia and said, "After a while, I knew I had to be with Lola. And she felt the same way. Then we got word about everything that was happening here. Lola was frantic about your injuries." Rory kept his face positioned so Lola could see his lips. She understood and nodded.

Then she had to join in so she began to sign. "When I heard what happened to you, I had to come home. I had to see you! But…" she paused. "Rory said no. So I didn't tell him and just flew into Madison two days ago."

Rory continued to explain that he found out what she was up to and was waiting for Lola at the airport when she arrived. Lydia bit her lip, thinking how Cade would have reacted to that.

"She won't do anything like that again, will you, babe?" Rory said with a meaningful look at Lola. She lowered her eyes and shook her head.

Lydia's eyes flashed when she realized what Rory had probably done to Lola and she was going to confront him, but Cade grabbed her and sat her back down.

Rory continued. "So I took her home with me and that's when Cade called to invite us up here." Rory got up and sat on his heels in front of Lydia. "Listen, Lydia. I love Lola. And she loves me. We want to work things out so we can live together. There's a lot of planning and rearranging of our lives that needs to be done, but I can't let her go. Do you understand what I'm saying?"

Tears once again flooded Lydia's eyes. "I'm really so happy for you, but this is a pretty big shock," Lydia said as she went to sit in front of Lola. The sisters signed together for a long time. Then Lydia threw her arms around Lola and rocked with her.

"Are you okay with all of this, Lydia? I know Lola wants you to be okay with it—and so do I," Rory said hopefully.

"I am thrilled Lola has found love." She threw her arms around Rory and kissed his cheek.

Cade stood and said, "This calls for a celebration, or at least a few beers."

Next to her wedding day, this was one of the happiest days of Lydia's life.

Chapter 30

The two couples spent a wonderful day together. The weather was perfect for boating and Cade and Rory showed the twins how much fun it was to be dragged behind the boat on a giant inflatable. They giggled and screamed in delight. Lydia couldn't remember the last time she and her sister had so much fun together.

Later in the day, Connor and Sarah arrived for the weekend. As Rory, Lola, Lydia and Cade were sharing the large double cabin, Connor and Sarah occupied one of the single ones nearby. It was so great having everyone so close together. The girls spent the late afternoon preparing a sumptuous feast while the guys got ready to grill out. Sarah had brought some Old-Fashioned Slush that was delicious but a little stronger than the twins were used to. After two drinks, things were getting a little loud and silly in the kitchen. When loud music joined the giggles and loud talking, Cade went to check it out.

Each of the girls had a glass of slush in one hand, clearly not their first, as they danced and laughed. When Sarah saw Cade come in, she ignored his annoyed expression and jumped up on the table to ask him to join her in a dance. At this, Lydia and Lola, suddenly more sober, worried how Cade would react. They didn't have long to wait.

"Sarah, get down from there now!" he said sternly and then directed his angry look at Lydia and Lola. "Give me those drinks, you two." They handed them over and he took a taste. "Christ, how much brandy is in here? Sarah, did you bring this stuff?" Cade emptied the twins' drinks into the sink and went to help Sarah off the table, but she argued with him, saying she was just dancing and he should lighten up.

Lydia actually gasped at her friend's behavior, but Sarah continued, "You're not the boss of me, Cade McCauley. Turn up the music, Lydia."

Lydia thought Cade was going to explode, but just as he made a move to grab Sarah off the table, Connor stormed through the door. "Well, I *am* the boss of you, Sarah DiCianni. Get the hell off that table now!"

Sarah took more risks than Lydia did, and Connor always seemed more willing to accept sassy behavior than Cade, meaning she was less likely to get spanked, so Lydia had to admit she was intrigued to see what was going to happen.

There was a short standoff as Connor held his hand out to Sarah so she could climb down. She waited a moment, but then rolled her eyes and took his hand. Lydia was sure that if she and Cade were in this situation, she would be in serious trouble. Connor and Sarah were different, but Lydia wasn't sure she had ever seen him so mad. Connor grabbed her arm and led her down the hall to the bedroom, and they could hear Connor's raised voice, but they could not hear Sarah talking back and there were no familiar spanking sounds.

"Let's eat," said Cade. Without asking, he poured glasses of ice water for the twins and said, "That concoction Sarah brought is way too strong for you, Lydia. I don't want to see you drinking it again. Do you understand?"

Rory added, "You can sign that to Lola as well." Lydia

signed what Cade had said while Rory gave Lola a stern look. Both girls nodded and went back to eating quietly.

Sarah and Connor came out in about ten minutes, and though Sarah blushed some when Connor made her apologize for bringing the strong slush and for sassing Cade, it didn't seem like her consequences were at all severe. Lydia thought she might be a little jealous.

As they lay in bed after making love that night, Cade explained that sometimes he thought Sarah was a bad influence on her and Lola and that while he understood she had no idea how strong the Old-Fashioned Slush was, she needed to remember how he felt about her drinking too much. He lectured her sternly, explaining that if he had come in to find her on the table, she would have found herself hauled off the table, taken to a bedroom and spanked until she couldn't sit for days.

Lydia nodded seriously while she battled with the tingle of desire she always got when he talked to her this way—even if she really didn't want the punishment.

When Lydia woke around 5:00 am, she realized Cade wasn't there. She was just going to look for him when he came back into the bedroom fully dressed. "What are you doing?" she asked sleepily. He sat down next to her and explained that it was raining lightly and the forecast had it raining until about noon. Connor loved to fish and these were perfect conditions, so they were going out for a few hours. Cade leaned down to kiss Lydia and when she greeted the kiss with a passionate groan, he yanked off the quilt covering her and made short work of his belt and pants. Lydia smiled in anticipation as he moved her nightgown up past her breasts. In his deep, rumbly voice, she heard him say, "What have we here? You know the rule about no panties in my bed." He drew them down her legs and off, then turned her to administer six spanks. "You know you've been naughty, don't you?"

"Yes, sir," she said as her breath hitched.

He turned her completely over onto her tummy and spanked lightly until she was whimpering and her bottom was a stingy pink. Then he lifted her hips to position his ready cock at her entrance. Before continuing, he reached between her folds to find her clit just waiting for him, and as he stroked it, Lydia began to moan louder and her breathing became more rapid. "Oh, Cade, please," she begged.

"Who's in charge here, little girl?"

"Oh, you are. You are. Please, Cade."

He knew his large, rough finger moving over her clit was bringing her close to the edge. Cade gauged when the time was right, removed his finger and entered her with a growl. Lydia grabbed a pillow to muffle her scream and they both climaxed together as he thrust into her a little more roughly than he planned. "Christ, Lydia, you drive me crazy!" Cade ground out as Lydia met each of his slowing moves. Finally, still inside her, he pulled her body into a spoon and wrapped his arms around her while their bodies calmed.

"Oh, Cade, that was so... so... so magical. I love you so much."

"I love you too, babe," he said as he kissed her neck and shoulders and pulled out of her. He got a warm cloth, cleaned her up and then himself, and got dressed. "I've got to go, Lydia. The guys will wonder where I am." She giggled as he kissed her forehead. Then tapping her nose, he said, "We'll be back in a few hours. Be good!"

"M'kay," she answered in a little girl voice as she snuggled back down under the warm covers.

Chapter 31

I t was a dark, rainy morning with the guys gone fishing, so the girls slept quite late. It was about 11:00 when they gathered in the kitchen of the big cabin for coffee and some breakfast.

The sun was peeking out by noon, and soon after, the day began to warm up. The guys had said they would be home by noon and maybe they would gas up the jet skis for the afternoon. The girls put their suits on and put some snacks together as they waited. Lydia and Lola had suits that were sexy but still one piece that worked out better for tubing, skiing, or jet skiing. Besides, Cade was pretty strict about Lydia not showing much flesh unless they were alone. So when Sarah came out in barely-there bikini in which she was able to show off her perfect body, Lydia was reminded again of how different Sarah's relationship with Cade's brother was. She wondered what Connor would think.

Noon passed, and it was drawing up at 1:30. The phone signals were spotty around the lake so the phones had no signals. The girls were all anxious to get out on the water, but Lydia thought the fish must have been biting and was thinking about the dinner they would make around fresh perch that night.

Sarah, however, was mad. "Where are they? I'm not spending this day stuck here inside making food. I was really looking forward to jet skiing or boating." She tried calling, but there was still no signal. "Goddammit, this really makes me mad!" Sarah was pacing around the cabin now and finally, she said, "You know what! If they are not back by 2:00, I am taking the boat ski out! Who's with me?"

The twins looked at each other and Lola signed, "Rory would not want me to go without him. I know you're disappointed, Sarah, but we have to wait. They'll be back soon."

But Sarah had worked herself up into a snit and burst out, "Oh, you two! Rory won't let me... Cade says no..." she said in a mocking sing song. "You two act like it's the 1950s!"

Lola took offence at this and stomped off to their bedroom. Lydia turned away and went back to slicing up vegetables. Sarah was angry now. She yanked the patio screen right out of its track, swore, and then just left it. "I'm not waiting any longer. Connor can't do this to me. I'll take the boat out myself! Don't try to stop me!"

Lydia picked up the broken screen and propped it against the wall while watching Sarah stomp down to the beach. Lola came down and asked what was going on. "Sarah is fit to be tied that the guys aren't back yet. She says she's taking the boat out herself."

Lola signed, "Isn't that dangerous?"

Lydia paused and said, "Yes, it is. She doesn't know anything at all about boats or handling them." By now Sarah was almost to the dock. Lydia made a decision. She turned to Lola and told her, "I'm going to try to talk her out of this, but if I can't, I have to go with her. I can't let her out on the lake alone." Lydia began running down the path, calling to Sarah to wait.

Lola started to run after her, but Lydia stopped and said, "No, Lola, you stay here so the guys know where we are. I will try to talk her out of going or at least into coming back quickly. I don't want you coming along."

Lola signed, "Cade is going to be really mad, you know."

"I know," Lydia called over her shoulder.

Sarah was already in the boat and had started the engine before Lydia hastily unhooked the dock lines and jumped in.

"Do you know how much trouble we are in?" Lydia yelled above the sound of the motor.

"I don't care!" Sarah yelled as she tried to back away from the dock. Lydia pushed her out of the way and took over. They left Lola helplessly standing on the deck watching the boat and her sister disappear. She was worried about what might happen out on the water and what would surely happen when Cade got ahold of her. A tear slipped down Lola's cheek.

Forty-five minutes later, Lola heard the sound of a boat pulling up and looked out to see the guys returning from fishing. They, of course, saw that the ski boat wasn't there. They raced up to the cabin, Cade in the lead. The first thing he saw was that the screen had been broken off its track. The second thing he saw was Lola wringing her hands with tears in her eyes.

"What happened? Where are Lydia and Sarah?" Cade thundered. There was no one to sign for Lola, but Rory had been doing a good job learning how to communicate with her with some signs and reading lips.

"Stop yelling at her, Cade, this isn't her fault and she is already upset," said Rory protectively. Then he gave Lola a hug and held her away so she could see his face. "What can you tell me about where Sarah and Lydia are?" It took a long time to get the story out and Cade and Connor were pacing and getting more and more agitated. Finally, they understood that Sarah was angry about waiting for them to get back and wanted to set off on the boat herself. Lydia didn't want her to go alone, so she went along. Lola tried to placate Cade by explaining that Lydia had tried to stop Sarah. It was now about an hour since they left and she pointed in the direction they had gone.

Cade grabbed his phone and began to try Lydia's number when he saw Lola holding Lydia's and Sarah's phones. They had left them. "Goddammit to hell!" said Connor and Cade in unison. "How much help did Lydia think she could be? She doesn't know her way around this lake," yelled Connor.

"Look, at least she knows how to drive the boat. This is Sarah's fault! She is hotheaded, sassy, and doesn't listen to you at all, Connor. You've got to take that girl in hand. You are way too easy on her."

Connor was mad. "Shut up, Cade. It's not like Lydia never gets in trouble. Let's address the problem at hand. How are we going find them?"

Just as they were heading back down to the dock to figure things out, they heard the sound of a boat and, looking up, saw a large ski boat driven by a couple of good-looking young guys towing the McCauley boat, with Lydia and Sarah in it. Relief filled Cade and Connor but was quickly replaced with anger. Still, they helped both boats get secured to the moorings. The girls' "rescuers" turned out to be teenagers from a property across the lake. They had come across Lydia and Sarah stranded about a mile away from the cabin. The boys could see that Cade and Connor were not in a chatting mood so they explained that they thought maybe the girls' boat had flooded or run out of gas and they didn't know where they were, but as they were pretty hot to get back, they just brought them. "Everyone knows the McCauley place and we were pretty close," one of the boys offered.

Cade pulled himself together to thank the boys and offer

them a fifty he took out of his pants pocket. They politely refused but Cade persuaded them that they really had helped them out. He thanked them, assured them that everything was fine, and slipped the ropes holding their boat off the dock. Lydia and Sarah, who had been noticeably quiet, called out a thank you and turned to face Cade and Connor whose expressions did not bode well.

"What the fuck are you wearing, Sarah?" was the first thing Connor said. Lydia had never heard him talk like that and it was clear Sarah hadn't, either. She looked up at him, bit her lip and said nothing.

"Have you lost your fucking minds?" yelled Cade, who was apparently also mad enough to use rare profanity. Cade grabbed Lydia out of the boat, walked a ways with a death grip on her arm and gave her a little shake. Then he put his mouth near her ear and said, "You are in serious trouble, little girl. You get up to that bedroom, put your nose in the corner and bare that bottom while you wait for me. Do you understand?" Lydia nodded as Cade reached back and gave her three tremendous swats as he sent her on her way. Not only did they sting like crazy, but she was also so embarrassed. Cade had never even threatened to spank her, much less do it, in front of anyone before. She was humiliated.

Lydia rushed to comply, not wanting to push any more of his buttons, and by the time he came up, she was in the corner with just a t-shirt on. Her little white bottom was positioned out just enough to make her think more about getting a spanking. She was sobbing softly.

Chapter 32

"**C**ome here, Lydia," he said as he sat on the bed. He drew her between his legs and immediately positioned her over one of his huge thighs. He pulled her close to him, grabbed her free hand to prevent it from protecting her bottom, and held her legs with his other leg. She was well and truly trapped in a spanking position.

"Oh please, Cade, I'm sorry. Really, I am!"

"I suppose you are, but you are going to be whole lot sorrier," he said as he heard her whimper. "I don't know the whole story, but I know enough to know that you did something dangerous, sneaky, and very naughty. I want to be sure you *never* do anything like this again." He laid his hand on her bottom and continued. "I am going to spank this fanny until it is cherry red and then I'm going to use this paddle to spank your thighs." He held the implement in front of her face, and now she was bawling. "When your thighs are sporting red welts, I'm going to spread your bright red cheeks open and put a naughty girl plug in you. Maybe this will make an impression on you."

Lydia's crying got louder. This was going be very painful!

And while his words made her damp with desire, it did not compete with the dread she felt at what was about to happen.

Then he started with very hard spanks from the very beginning. He spanked for a long time and she was gulping for air. He stopped for a few moments but started up again. That happened three times. Then he paused and said, "I'm going to paddle your thighs now and it's going to hurt a lot. I want you to think about this paddle the next time you decide to do something foolish with Sarah. Understand?" Then he grabbed a pillow, handed it to her and said, "You may need this, baby."

And oh, she did. Lydia screamed as the first paddle stroke hit her thighs and kept screaming into the pillow until he stopped. By now, she was lying limp across his leg, having given in to the pain. She knew better than to try to get up.

Before she completely caught her breath, she felt his lubricated finger push into her butt. He moved it in and out of her anus a few times and then she felt the plug pushing up inside her. It was so much bigger than the last one.

"Cade, please, I can't! It's too big! Please!" she cried.

"It's just a little bigger than the last one and you can take it. Bear down—now!" Lydia did as she was told and Cade seated the plug all the way in. It hurt, but more than that, it felt uncomfortable and humiliating. "Good girl. You are going to keep that in until I say it can come out. It will help you think about what you did today to deserve this punishment." He sat her up on his lap then and wiped off her face. He held her briefly before he said, "Now you take that sore red bottom with the naughty girl plug back over to the corner—nose on the wall and butt sticking out. And don't even think about rubbing the sting away. You think about how you look and how you feel and see if you ever want this to happen again. Understand me, Lydia?"

"Yes, sir."

"I'm going down to get the boat secured. You stay right there."

Lydia was thoroughly miserable. It was the hardest and most embarrassing spanking he had ever given her and she felt terrible that she had disappointed him. She started out being mad at Sarah, but she had gone along with her when she didn't need to. She knew Cade would say this was her decision and her problem and he would always hold her accountable.

By the time he came back, Lydia was still sniffling and hiccuping a little, but she was also shivering. Cade grabbed the soft throw off the bed, wrapped it around her and carried her back to the bed to sit with her on his lap. He rocked her and kissed her until he heard her breathing become even. She had fallen asleep. He laid her down on her tummy and covered her gently. Then he went downstairs to see how Connor had fared with Sarah.

Connor had always been more easy-going than Cade, and as adults, when he watched his brother's relationship with his new sister-in-law, he thought of him as even more intense. He was a little surprised that Cade had found a woman who would not only put up with his 'I'm-in-charge' attitude but seemed to thrive on it. Cade had been lucky to find Lydia.

But when Connor saw Sarah the first time at the Home for Everyone building site helping Lydia work with hearing-impaired students, he was blown away. Her long blonde hair, brown eyes and dimples would have been enough, but even in work clothes, he could see she had a knockout body. And she had proven to be full of personality—fun loving, smart and delightfully irreverent. He was attracted to her almost instantly. Cade had warned him off, saying she would be 'difficult to tame' and that she was 'too wild.' Yet Connor liked those things about her too. Sarah and Lydia were very different people yet had become fast and loyal friends. He thought they complemented each other well. Where Cade took his role to guide and protect Lydia very seriously, Connor was generally content to let Sarah be her own girl. Then he fell in love. That changed things.

As Connor came to care about Sarah very much, he felt the need to keep her near him and safe. He cared about how she acted in front of other guys, how much she drank and how much leg she was showing in the short skirts she favored. He tried to rein her in the way he had watched his brother do with Lydia, but Sarah resisted being told what to do. Connor was frustrated.

For her part, Sarah had always prided herself on her independence and her sort of tough demeanor. She was raised with four older brothers who allowed her to be a tomboy and run with them, until she was suddenly a young woman and they tried to make her change. She wasn't having it. She could drink, swear and carouse with them with barely a hangover. Boys in high school and college had found her 'too much to handle' and she was fine with that until she met Connor. Sweet, fun, easy-going, beautiful Connor! But now she didn't know how to act. She was afraid he would never go for her. She was shocked when he seemed more and more interested in her. She felt herself falling in love but was not sure how to make a man happy.

Connor worked up the courage to ask Sarah out a few weeks after he met her at the construction site. They had a great time together. He found her so full of life and fun that he was willing to overlook the fact that she often drank a little too much and slipped into profanity once in a while. She was a risk taker and he liked that about her.

But that changed on the day Sarah helped Lydia lie and sneak away while Lydia was still recovering from being attacked by Senator Jacobi. That time, she had crossed a line and when the girls finally arrived home from their clandestine adventure, Connor had been as prepared as Cade to spank his girl into next week. That changed the trajectory of their relationship and though Sarah's personality remained the same, she knew the consequences if she pushed Connor too far by risking her health or safety.

There was no way he could let this boat incident slide. She had acted like a toddler having a tantrum and put herself and her friend in danger. And she knew she was in trouble. Sarah said nothing as Connor dragged her back to their cabin and made her last spanking seem like a walk in the park. He didn't even begin with his hand but picked up a paddle and used it until she went limp over his lap. Her mottled and throbbing backside looked incredibly painful and Sarah was sobbing loudly. Connor held her there, though, and explained to her that her spanking was over, but her punishment was not. Taking an idea from Cade's playbook, he kept Sarah over his knee while he showed her a plug he planned to use to take her punishment up a level. As he suspected, Sarah had never seen a plug or heard of one, but when he explained that he would be parting her bottom cheeks to insert this up into her, she wailed. He waited her out, put lube on the plug and explained to her what he was doing. She didn't fight him off, but she clenched her cheeks so much, he had to put down the plug, administer a few spanks and start over. He finally got the pacifier-like plug in position so that he could just see it peeking out of her bottom, and he had to admit it was a huge turn on. But now was not the time to act on that. He lightly rubbed her back as he explained that she would keep that plug in until he said it could come out and she was to let it remind her *never* to pull a stunt like she had today.

He pulled her up then to sit on his lap, wiped her face, and waited for her to calm down. He held her for quite a while as crying and apologizing faded.

"I'm going to get you a bottle of water and then I need you lie down for a while. Nap if you can."

Sarah almost argued with him, but damn if that plug didn't remind her to behave. "Okay," she said meekly.

"I'll come and get you when dinner is ready."

Connor made his way to the bedroom door.

"Connor?" Sarah called in a watery voice. "Do you still love me? I mean, can you love me when I've been so ... so—"

"Naughty?" he suggested. Connor came back to sit next to her. He pushed her hair off her tear-streaked face and kissed her lips lightly. "Oh, baby, I am in so deep! You'll never be rid of me."

Sarah smiled and was asleep in minutes.

Chapter 33

Rory had decided it would be a good idea to take Lola to the farmer's market in town that afternoon, as the mood around the cabins was not pleasant. Cade and Connor left Lydia and Sarah to sulk in their bedrooms after their epic spankings. The brothers were going to clean fish for dinner and cut some firewood in the afternoon, and though they were not sorry to have punished them, they hoped by dinnertime, the girls would be willing to join them.

When Lydia awoke, she was immediately reminded that she had a sore bottom with a punishment plug inserted. She blushed, even though she was alone. She wanted that plug out but knew she had to wait for Cade to allow it. She awoke when she heard Cade get into the shower. When he came out completely naked, with water droplets still clinging to his tan and muscular body, Lydia scolded herself for the desire she felt and the dampness between her legs when she still couldn't even roll over on her backside and that infernal plug was so humiliating! She pretended to be sleeping but watched him through her lashes. He put on clean black jeans and a black t-shirt that did nothing to hide his physique. Honestly, she had to control her breathing.

"I see you're awake, little girl," he said, smiling.

She said nothing and wouldn't smile but knew he would not stand for prolonged petulance. Finally, she said, "I heard you in the shower."

Cade came to sit down next to her on the bed. Her face could not disguise the fact that she probably had cried herself to sleep and she was sleeping on her tummy. "Let me get that naughty girl plug out of you."

She pouted and turned her head away from him but said, "Yes, please."

He lifted the covers and what he saw made him immediately hard. Lydia's silken black hair lay in a tangled mess around her head and back. The only clothing she wore was a short pink t-shirt, as he had stripped her from the waist down. Her heart-shaped bottom was still red and swollen, had some fading welts and he could also see the end of the "pacifier" peeking out from inside her. He allowed himself a few moments and finally she said, "Please take it out, Cade. My bottom hurts."

"Well, it's supposed to hurt, babe. Do you think you learned your lesson?"

"Yes, sir."

"Get up on your knees and keep your head down. I'll get it out."

Lydia did as he asked and, again, he took a moment to enjoy the picture she made with that naughty bottom now up in the air waiting for relief. He couldn't help but check to see if she was aroused. He pushed one finger inside her and was not disappointed. He coated his fingers with her liquid and used that essence to lubricate the plug before popping it out. He lifted her then and brought her to his lap, holding her carefully so she was not sitting directly on his rough jeans. "Feeling better, baby?"

"A little. But, Cade, I don't know if I can sit."

"Well, we're going to have dinner soon and you will join us —sitting. Feeling a spanking for a long while is part of the deal, as you know. I am not going to argue about it. Get yourself ready and dressed. I need you to put together that good breading you make for the fish. Then I'll fry them. Got it?"

Cade's phone rang just as they were finishing the dinner clean up. He answered and Lydia heard him say, "What? What?" Pause. "In front of the judge?" Pause. "All of them?" Pause. "It's hard to believe. What does this all mean?"

Now Lydia had come to stand in front of Cade, who pulled her to his side. The conversation continued in the same way until finally, he said, "Goddammit, Jackson! This is great news!" Then, "Yeah, we're all up at our family cabins in Eagle River. What do you have going tomorrow? Why don't you and Anita drive up here? You could explain this all to Connor and the girls. You'd do a better job than I can." Then, "No, stay here, we have an extra cabin you can stay in—it's all set for you. If it's nice, we can take the boat out." Then, "That sounds great! We'll see you tomorrow!"

Cade called out, "Hey, everyone! Get in here! I have news!" Then he grabbed Lydia and bent her backwards for a drama kiss.

"Cade, stop, what's happening?" She laughed.

When everyone was in the kitchen, Cade began, "That was Jackson Graves. He said they had what they thought would be a plea deal meeting with Jacobi, the lawyers, and the judge. It seems the senator had a come-to-Jesus moment, began to cry and confessed to all the sexual harassment, assaults and even two rapes—in front of the judge and defense lawyers!"

Lydia was busy signing Cade's words for Lola, but Sarah burst out, "Oh my God! Oh my God! Does this mean it's over? Completely over?"

"Well, I invited Jackson and Anita up here tomorrow, to explain all the details. He said he has never heard of this happening but thinks it can only be good for the victims."

Lydia finished signing for Lola, who threw her arms around her and began to cry. Sarah joined the hug, saying, "I'm so happy for you! This is such wonderful news!"

There was much backslapping, hugging and kissing. Then Lola asked for their attention. She signed while Lydia interpreted, "This day began so sadly. How could it turn out so happy?"

Rory grabbed Lola and said, "Well said, baby. Well said." Then he surprised everyone by giving her a deep and meaningful kiss.

Lydia looked up at Cade with tears in her eyes and said, "It's almost more than I can take!"

Chapter 34

Jackson and Anita would be up at the cabin after lunch, so the couples had plenty of time to sleep late and eat leisurely breakfasts. Rory and Lola took the kayak out, Connor took Sarah to see the Cathedral of the Pines in the nearby state forest, and Cade and Lydia took a long walk around the lake talking to old neighbors who had known Cade's father and grandfather.

Cade heard Lydia sniffle and looked down to see tears in her eyes. He stopped and held her face. "What's the matter, baby?"

"This is just all so beautiful. I never knew life could be this way. Here I am, with the man I love, in this heavenly place—and my sister and best friend are here too. I just think I am going to wake up and it will all go away." And then she began to cry.

Cade was reminded how sensitive and loving his Lydia was as he put her arms around her. "I feel the same way, Lydia McCauley. I am so happy to be making memories with you here at this cabin that means so much to me. I love you, baby." And he kissed her tears away.

Anita and Jackson arrived at midday when the sun was bright and the temperature was perfect. Lydia thought she had never seen a sky more blue. They were so impressed with the family cabin compound and the grounds and thanked Cade, over and over, for the invitation. The girls set out a charcuterie board and served beer, wine and water and they sat around the table on the deck to hear Jackson and Anita tell them what had happened to Senator Jacobi.

Jackson explained that the senator had decided he absolutely did not want to go to trial. His lawyers told him that their independent pretrial investigation indicated that his odds of winning at trial were slim, but that winning was the only way this could possibly go away. He still said no. The senator was advised that considering the number of women who had come forward, the seriousness of his offences, and the fact that he involved the Office of Special Services in the crimes and cover-up, made him almost impossible to defend. It didn't help that he had also tried to flee the country. This made Jacobi's choices in a plea deal difficult, but that's what he wanted to do. So there are a few complicated scenarios that could play out because he didn't want a trial and consequences vary from him doing prison time and going on the sex offender registry to him getting probation.

"Probation?" Cade exploded. "He raped two women, assaulted and harassed a dozen more and nearly killed my wife! And he could get probation?" Jackson stood and immediately continued.

"Wait, Cade! I know how that sounds, but please let me finish."

Cade sat down and Lydia went to stand next to him. He drew her onto his lap.

Jackson continued. "So, keep in mind that his political career is definitely over. Also, I can tell you that I think most judges would recommend throwing the book at Jacobi, but

Judge Hunter is the judge who drew this case. He is known for being very hard on sex offenders and also has no time for politicians. The fact that he was the chosen judge was some good news that I wanted to bring up to you today, but it gets better. On my way up here, my assistant called and said that the judge called the attorneys and the defendant in today and announced that the only plea deal he would accept was a sentence reduction from twenty years to fifteen years with parole eligibility in ten years. He will also be on the sex offender registry for life. To have his sentence reduced even this much, he must flip on the administrator of the Office of Special Services who was assisting Senator Jacobi and two other state employees who were recruiting young women for the purpose of sex.

Anita spoke up. "Cade, I know you would like to see much worse happen to the senator, but Jackson says that the severity of his sentence is more than we could have ever gotten if Lydia and the others had not spoken up."

"That's right. The stars aligned when Lydia and the others found Anita and she did her thing. All of them deserve a lot of credit. Jacobi is a broken man now, with no future. He will never hurt a woman again. This is a rare victory."

"I know you're right, Jackson. I owe you both a lot for tackling this case and seeing it through. You've done a great job. Thank you." Then he paused and added, "Why don't you let me take you all out to eat tonight to celebrate? I'll make reservations at Botolotti's Cin Cin—you'll love it. It's time to celebrate!"

"Isn't that sort of a fancy place, Cade? We don't have anything to wear. Do we have time to go into town to shop? I think I saw some boutiques advertised," said Sarah.

"You don't want to come out on the boat?" Connor asked.

The girls all looked at each other and then Lola made a sign like scales weighing things out. Lydia interpreted, "Let's see, going on a boat or buying a fancy dress for a celebration? Hmm!"

The girls all laughed, but Cade was still nervous about letting Lydia out of his sight.

"All right. But I want to see your charged phone on you before you leave and you will be back by 5:00 pm or there will be hell to pay. Reservations are for 7:30. Got it, Lydia?"

"I got it, Cade," she said, careful not to sound sassy.

"Lydia! Girls! Come on! We'll miss our reservations!" Cade called out from the great room.

"Just a minute. We're almost ready," Sarah called back.

The girls had had so much fun finding sexy dresses and shoes for tonight, and then they'd fussed with each other's hair and makeup when they got back. As they got ready, Lydia watched Sarah. When choosing dresses earlier, Sarah had gone straight to the ultra-sexy ones with low fronts, and backs, that were also short and designed to show off curves. Lydia knew that Cade would never allow her to wear anything like that and she wondered if Connor would be bothered by Sarah's choice. But that was them and not really her business. So Lydia was surprised when Sarah pulled her dress out of the bag and it was lovely and actually modest, by Sarah standards.

Sarah saw Lydia looking at her dress quizzically. "You know, Lydia," she said, "I decided I don't want to egg Connor on. I'm pretty sure he would be more comfortable if I wore something that was not so, well, not so revealing. I never thought I would let a man influence what I wore but... well... I want Connor to be happy with me. He's really a great guy, a little bossy but not as bad as Cade," she said as she rolled her eyes." She paused then, looked at Lydia and said, "I'm pretty sure I am in love with your brother-in-law, Lydia, and if I have to "mind him"—she made air quotes—I will. I love him."

"I'm so happy," said Lydia as she gave Sarah a great big hug. "Now let's go knock their socks off!"

They were happy with the results of their afternoon of work so they decided to make a dramatic entrance coming down the stairs into the great room of the cabin. As they made their way slowly down the stairs, the guys looked up and what they saw took their breath away. Each of the girls looked stunning. Lydia waited for Cade to complain about the length of her dress, but instead he said, "You look just beautiful, babe!"

Jackson took Anita's hand and spun her around, making a wolf whistle, and Rory signed, "You are so beautiful," to Lola. Everyone looked to Connor, who took Sarah's arm, moved a few steps away and whispered something into her ear. No one could hear, but Sarah blushed profusely.

Cade had secured a large booth in a private corner of the supper club and encouraged them to order whatever they wanted, on his tab. They ate, drank, laughed and had a spectacular time together. Then as the wait staff cleared their plates to make room for dessert, Connor stood and moved to kneel next Sarah's chair.

"Connor, stop. What are you doing? Get up!" Sarah cried, growing bright red from embarrassment.

There was a hush in the dining room as Connor said, "The first day I saw you, I knew you were the woman for me. You are funny, smart, sassy and there's no one more beautiful. I want to spend my life with you, Sarah DiCianni. Will you be my wife?"

Sarah's hands had gone to her mouth in amazement and as tears filled her eyes, she said, "Oh yes, yes, a million times, yes! I love you, Connor McCauley!"

The entire room erupted in applause and cheers, and the

couple stood as he placed the ring on her finger and spun her around. Two waiters appeared and popped the corks on champagne bottles as the couple engaged in a passionate kiss.

Much later, as they lay in each other's arms, Lydia sighed, thinking back on the momentous day. Wistfully, she said, "Oh, Connor was so romantic tonight."

"Yeah, I didn't know he had it in him," Cade said with a chuckle.

"Do you think I am funny, smart and beautiful?"

"Absolutely, baby. And you know what else? You are the bravest woman I have ever known. Your courage throughout this entire ordeal has amazed me. You are one of a kind and don't you ever forget that, Lydia McCauley. I love you!"

Hannah Kane

Hannah Kane dove right into writing with her first romance series, *Love Signs*. The first book, *Signs of Love* was released in August 2021 with others - *Signs of Courage* and *Signs of Hope* - following later in the year.

Hannah believes the gift of story came from her mother and was so deeply instilled that she became a children's librarian and professional storyteller.

Hannah now spends her days working part time in a crisis center, enjoying family and friends in the comfort of the lakeside neighborhood where she grew up, and of course, happily writing romance.

Don't miss these exciting titles by Hannah Kane and Blushing Books!

Love Signs
Signs of Love
Signs of Courage
Signs of Hope (December 2021)

Blushing Books

Blushing Books is the oldest eBook publisher on the web. We've been running websites that publish steamy romance and erotica since 1999, and we have been selling eBooks since 2003. We have free and promotional offerings that change weekly, so please do visit us at http://www.blushingbooks.com/free.

Blushing Books Newsletter

Please join the Blushing Books newsletter
to receive updates & special promotional offers.
You can also join by using your mobile phone:
Just text **BLUSHING** to 22828.

Every month, one new sign up via text messaging will receive
a $25.00 Amazon gift card, so sign up today!